Queen of Vampires

Her Protectors

Lina Bengston

Published by Lina Bengston, 2021.

QUEEN OF VAMPIRES

First edition. July 1, 2021.

Copyright © 2021 Lina Bengston.

ISBN: 978-1735549231

Written by Lina Bengston.

Table of Contents

Prologue

I brushed the hair off my face in irritation. "These meetings are becoming more tedious."

Jarius cupped my face, then tucked the remaining strands of hair behind my ear and said, "Be patient, my love. Soon, we'll have our long-awaited retirement in the cabin."

Looking for reassurance, I gazed back into his eyes as I felt Duncan's warm embrace and tender lips press on my cheek. I sighed in comfort and looked at my mates in gratitude. *I wouldn't know what to do if they weren't by my side.*

Gadiel took my hand and threaded our fingers together as he led me down the hall while Nikolas kept hold of my left hand.

My mouth curved into a tired smile as we made our way out of the Lavania mansion, deep in the Casters' property. "I'm glad you're all here with me," I said with a sigh. The meeting dragged on while I anxiously awaited to get back home since I had a nagging feeling I was needed back at Vampire territory.

The Rulers' Consortium meetings were randomly assigned the night before, and the location was not pre-planned for safety measures. Casters from each race bound us with unbreakable spells that each ruler must take before joining the Consortium. This spell prevented us from harming each other during our meeting.

Our footsteps echoed through the empty hall as we made our way to the front. Then, I felt a sudden drop in energy. My steps faltered, and I tightened my grip on my mates' hands, but by the time the stairs that would lead us down to the car were in sight, Gadiel and Jarius were holding most of my weight up. I took in deep, slow breaths while Jarius covered my front and Duncan my back so no one would see me in my weakened state.

Is it the princess? Jarius asked through our link.

I gritted my teeth as I focused on staying upright. Instead of answering, I dropped my barrier.

Gadiel's grip around my waist tightened when he read my thoughts and registered the level of my power. *I hate seeing you this way*, he projected.

Jarius, get us out of here, Nikolas snapped.

Jarius' back tensed, and his fists clenched. *You know I can't do that. It's against the rules.*

I felt Duncan's distress before he sent out, *Fuck the rules. We can explain later. She is vulnerable in this state, and she can't be out in the open.*

I agree, Gadiel responded.

I hated it when they worried about me. With a shaky hand, I brushed the sweat off my face and said, *I'm fine. It will pass soon enough. Let's not break any rules. We're close to the boundary line, then Jarius can take us back home.*

We all descended the stairs at a brisk pace, which had me breaking out into a sweat from the effort not to show any weakness, or my enemies would strike.

Halfway down, Jarius took off to get the car. By the time we made it to the bottom, he was already jumping out of the driver's side and opening the back door for me.

As soon as they secured me behind the tinted windows, I let out a deep breath and laid my head back with my eyes closed.

My successor must have had another power surge—which had been happening more frequently over the past year. The power transfer was getting close, which meant she would soon take over.

Every time she used her powers, it zapped me of mine. The sudden drop had been jarring, especially when it happened at an inappropriate time. With a sinking feeling my mind raced to what my next few months would look like. *I would need to limit my trips outside of the castle since I shouldn't be caught in a sudden energy drop out in the open.*

I shifted my weight as I felt the worry and frustration of my mates through our link. I knew what was coming; they had been asking me to bring in my successor sooner.

I placed my arm over my eyes to shield myself since I didn't have the energy to argue with them.

"It's time, Illeana," Jarius said.

I knew it! I took a moment, then I lifted my head and noted his rigid back and corded muscles as he tightly gripped the steering wheel. "Soon. Once she starts training, the surges will be more manageable."

"Until then, we should no longer leave the castle," Duncan interrupted from the front. His profile showed how hard he was clenching his jaw.

As weak as I was, I hated it when they were being overly protective, so I sat up to argue and noticed we were driving past the protective barrier of the mansion. But then, the car jerked, and it threw me to Nik, who wrapped his arms around me.

"What the fuck!" Jarius said.

"We're under attack! Nik, protect her." Duncan jumped out of the car, using his Vampire speed.

"Duncan, no. Get back in here." I looked back as we sped away and didn't notice Gadiel open the door next to me.

"Jarius, get her out!" Gadiel shouted as he followed Duncan.

"Goddammit! Stop the car. We need to help them."

"No. You're our priority. We need to get you to safety." Nik's arms tightened around me as he yelled, "What the fuck is taking so long, Jarius?"

"I can't. They have a spell preventing me from transporting us out of here." He responded through gritted teeth.

My Vampire sight trailed Duncan and Gadiel. "Then stop. We need to fight," I pleaded, glimpsing Jarius' glare from the rearview mirror.

Duncan and Gadiel were facing off with several creatures. "Stop. They're outnumbered." I screamed, but Nik and Jarius ignored me. Instead, I heard the engine roar as Jarius stepped on the gas.

That's it! I closed my eyes and took a deep calming breath as I pulled power from my people. It was something I reserved doing unless in the direst situations. I tensed as a surge of energy flooded inside of me, which restored me back to normal. This ability made the queen of Vampires a formidable opponent. I could tap into the collective minds of each Vampire and share their powers, which allowed our race to flourish and evolve.

Nik shook my shoulders. "Stop, Illeana. Don't do this," he pleaded. "We need to leave. We promise to come back and help them, but we need to get you to safety."

I ignored him as the power filled me to the brim, and my veins thrummed with different energies, eagerly waiting for my command.

The power saturating my body made my senses sharper and reflexes faster, so I didn't waste any time as I flashed to Duncan and Gadiel. Nik and Jarius sent out colorful curses through our mind link, followed by the tires' loud screeching from the sudden break.

I glanced at Duncan, who had control over life energy, as he pulled the life force of three creatures in front of him while Gadiel, who had control over emotions, had two writhing in pain. I looked around and noticed the other rulers and their men fighting not too far away.

The strange creatures had a horrible stench and had mismatched body parts made up of animals and supernaturals, making them look grotesque and scary. They were not of any race I recognized.

I raised my hand and opened up a massive hole in the ground that buried them, then waved my hand quickly as the ground knitted back together. This cleared the path so I could study my surroundings. Their numbers seemed endless, even as we dispatched several at a time.

Where are they coming from? I looked around and narrowed my eyes as I saw the creatures funnel in from an open portal toward the wooded area to the mansion's right.

I raced in the portal's direction, throwing energy balls at any creatures in my path, ignoring Gadiel and Duncan's calls.

Jarius and Nik joined my side just as I punched a seven-foot-tall creature standing on two legs. It had what looked like a rhino face and a long tusk, which went past his nose, black pitted eyes, and black liquid dripped from his sharp teeth. The creature flew backward and fell with a thud as I'd laced my punch with energy equivalent to a thunderbolt.

Jarius, a caster, and Nik, who controlled thoughts, cleared a path for me, so I made it to the portal faster.

More creatures poured through the opening.

I reached up to the sky, pulled lightning energy, then directed it to the portal.

I felt all four of my mates surround me as I worked on destroying the portal. I was confident they would protect me, so I focused all of my attention on the massive hole in front of me. The edges sparked as the portal's energy collided with mine—it felt dark, and it exuded pure evil, something I'd never felt before.

Fuck, it will require massive amounts of energy to close this thing.

Nikolas must have read my thoughts since I heard him project to the other rulers to close the portal. His mind control could tap into anyone's thoughts within the vicinity. He rarely used his powers against other races out of mutual respect; plus, it was against the rules, but this situation called for it.

I sensed the other rulers appear next to me. The human ruler, who had his own talents but didn't possess an active power, fought with us using his impressive offensive fighting skill. The Shifters were vicious fighters; they tore through the creature's limbs while the Fae used earth energy. The queen stood by my side, working on the portal along with her guards while her other men fought the creatures. The Casters worked with us as we combined our powers to destroy the portal.

"Katharina, try to direct all of our energies towards the center," I yelled through the noise, glancing at the head coven witch.

She nodded and started casting.

Aredhel, the Fae queen, made a fancy motion with her hands, and blue energy blasted toward the center.

I continued to have lightning blast at the portal while I pulled power from my surroundings and diverted it back.

Soon, the portal flickered, followed by a loud boom. Then the portal's energy blasted outward, which threw me a few feet away, where I landed on my back.

Sitting up with a groan, I noticed Katharina near me. However, Aredhel wasn't moving. I was about to go to her, but her men surrounded her immediately.

"Is she okay?" My brows knitted in concern.

"She is alive. We must take her home to cure her injuries," her first in command said, gesturing for his men to lift the queen.

"Take care of her and please keep us posted on her condition," Katharina said to their retreating backs.

"We should all head back. Our men should be able to handle the stragglers," Lucian, the Shifter's alpha, said with a furrowed brow as he looked around the destruction.

I followed his gaze to the uprooted trees that surrounded us, the scorch marks up and down the mansion path, and the small crater the portal left on the ground. A few men were still fighting, but overall, it had died down.

"We should get you home." Jarius placed his hand on my hip and nodded to the other rulers. We glanced at our other three mates and flashed back to the castle.

Chapter 1
Serris

As I bounded down the stairs, I smelled breakfast from the kitchen and found Mom over the stove, cooking sausage and eggs. "Good morning." I kissed her on the cheeks, to which she responded with a light pat on my face. Dad sipped his coffee and had a paper in front of him. After stopping to place a kiss on his cheek and hugging his back, I joined him at the breakfast table. "Morning, Dad." I picked a buttered toast from his plate and gulped down orange juice.

"Slow down there, Turbo. Why are you in a hurry?"

"Meeting up with the guys," I said in between bites.

"You don't want eggs?" Mom asked.

I shook my head and popped the last bite into my mouth, licking the yummy butter grease off my fingers.

Dad folded the paper in front of him and set his cup down. "What are you kids doing today?"

I shrugged. "The usual. Hang out, enjoy the summer." I balled up a napkin and got up to leave.

"Ser, stick with the guys, okay?" Dad said, like he always does before I leave the house.

"Yes, Dad," I said with an eye roll and started walking out of the kitchen.

"Have fun, sweetheart," Mom called.

"I will. Bye!"

9

I cruised on my moped past the other councils' mansions—there were seven of them, including my parents. Their houses were all in the gated community located in Awhil, a suburb outside of Abrea—The largest Vampire City globally. Abrea housed the queen's castle called The Crelan, which took up half of the town. When I come within miles of the castle my skin crawls because powerful wards surround it, making it impossible to bypass. The Crelan was centrally located to protect the queen—our beating heart.

The queen was a part of every Vampire, so we instinctively wanted to protect her. We called her our beating heart because, without her, the Vampire race would weaken. This was a guarded secret I only knew about because I overheard my parents talk about it one night. They almost made me swear on my first born just so I wouldn't share this knowledge with anyone. If the queen didn't exist, they said we would revert to our bestial ancestors—those who mindlessly drained blood of any beating heart.

My best friends were in the family council as well, therefore, lived on the compound. We were meeting at Kagan's home, down the block, past the other property's luscious green grounds.

I stopped in front of his gate and punched in the code. When I reached the front door, I strolled right in, not bothering to knock since we all grew up in each other's houses.

"Guys?"

"Hi, Serris," Mrs. Northwood greeted, coming down one of the double staircases.

"Hi."

"The boys are in Kagan's room."

"Thanks, Mrs. Northwood," I called over my shoulder as I ran up the stairs. I walked down the hall, all the way to the end. Kagan's room, took up the whole right wing of the mansion. Pausing in front of the door, I raised my hand and knocked, then I turned the knob when I heard the guys' voices through the door.

My eyes scanned the room and noticed the rumpled sheets on the extra-large king-size bed on the right—our parents switched out all of our mattresses to custom made super-king sizes since we alternated spending the night in each other's houses, and they got tired of making our individual beds. Now all five of us fit comfortably in the bed with room to spare since Godric liked to take up a big part of the bed while the twins loved to snuggle. Technically, I should feel weird sharing a bed with four boys, but we've been doing it since before we could crawl, so I'm used to it.

I glanced by the window, where I heard a beep from Kagan's three computer screens. "Hey, Ser," He called from behind the desk. Next to it was an entertainment center, a few bean bags were scattered next to the couch in front of a large screen TV where Godric smiled from the beanbag, a remote control in his hand.

I opened my mouth in greeting, but then I flinched as I had the wind knocked out of me as the twins threw their entire weight on me with their arms wrapped around my chest, then one of them started tickling my side. "Stop." I giggled and squirmed to detangle myself from them. Colin and Liam were very affectionate and playful. This was how they greeted me every time, no matter where we were, which was embarrassing when they did it in school.

I successfully freed myself and ran to Godric, who had his arms ready, as he was always saving me from the twins.

I sat in between his legs, where he caged me in his arms as he pressed the buttons on the remote.

The twins came at me, but I buried myself deeper into Godric's embrace.

He swatted on the twins' arms. "Quit it," he snapped.

I laughed and covered it up by burying my face in Godric's chest.

"Laugh it up, Ser. Godric can't keep you safe for long," Colin said.

"Yep. It's just a matter of time." Liam smirked with a sparkle of mischief in his eyes.

"Will you two give it a rest?" Kagan sighed as he got up from the computer desk and sat on the couch next to us. He was the more serious one and didn't touch me as much. Between the four, Kagan acted more like an older brother who always worried over our safety. He has always been a tad overprotective of me. Even when we were younger, he punched Godric, when we were just six years old because he made me cry.

On the other hand, Godric was quiet and grumpy, but he was more agreeable to the escapades the twins and I come up with.

The five of us grew up together—our parents were all in the council and were best friends. It was weird, but they all had children in the same year, so we had been inseparable since we were kids.

"What are we doing today, Kags?"

His eyes narrowed on Godric's arms around me before answering. "We just wanted to chill today."

"Speak for yourself. That sounds boring. How about we explore the lake?" Colin interjected.

I nodded my head to the idea.

"Can we please just stay in for once?" He leaned back heavily on the couch.

"What's wrong? You look tired." I got out of Godric's arms and sat next to Kagan, studying his hunched posture and tense shoulders.

He rubbed his eyes with the heel of his hands. "I had a long training session last night, and I'm tired."

I held in a frown in response to his words. The kids with active powers, like Kagan, needed extra training after school. We had regular curriculums in school to promote interspecies interaction, so the quad trained several times a week afterward.

I, on the other hand, didn't have extra powers. I only had the usual strength, speed, and resilience that any Vampire possessed. I was eagerly waiting for my true powers to manifest, but nothing yet. Sure, I'd shown signs of being able to read power, and I might have had some burst of energy come out of me when I was emotional, but all Vamps were capable of the same thing. My parents and the quad kept telling me to be patient, but I should have shown a hint of my powers already. It was a sore subject for me, and I didn't want to talk about it since I secretly feared I didn't have true power and I'd be the only Vamp without one.

"Why don't you go back to bed, and we can hang somewhere else?"

"Not a chance, who knows what you three would get into without me."

"Hey, what do you think of me?" Godric said as he lifted his controller and frantically pressed buttons to fire a gun at an alien.

The kids in school referred to my best friends as the quad; they were the most powerful kids our age. They had rare powers that manifested early. Godric could pull the life force out of someone. Something we discovered at a very young age. At eight, he protected me from a kid teasing me in school. He got so angry he pulled his life force, which almost killed the kid. He had been fearful since then of accidentally killing someone. It was that day that Godric had drawn into himself. He always has to have total control of his emotions, so he didn't say much—especially around others. On rare occasions, he would sometimes relax and break into a smile when he was around us.

"Still. I need to keep an eye on those three." Kagan sat deeper into the couch.

I bumped his shoulder with mine. "You need to relax some and stop worrying about us. We're fine."

He shook his head stubbornly.

"Yeah," Colin snorted.

I held in my annoyance. Admittedly, the twins and I had gotten into some trouble, but it was nothing too crazy to warrant his level of distrust. When we were ten, we took out the twins' father's boat and got stuck in the middle of the lake because we didn't think to check for gas, and there were no paddles. Kagan raised the alarm and told our parents. By the time they found us, there was a full-on search party looking for us. It had been dark and cold, but we weren't worried. We were Vampires, after all. Although we had the same bodily functions as humans, we were more resilient and had been confident someone would find us, so we enjoyed our time out in the lake and swam in the dark. Kagan and Godric were the ones who'd found us after about five hours.

Another time the twins and I went hiking outside of the compound and got lost. I wouldn't ever admit it to Kagan, but I was a little scared as we encountered a few wild animals. After several hours of walking, it exhausted me. It was a good thing Liam could manipulate feelings while Colin could control minds. However, they were still learning their powers, so their attempts didn't always go as planned.

Those weren't the only times we had gotten in trouble throughout the years, but nothing ever happened. The twins were filled with energy, which always led to mischief. They couldn't sit still or be contained in a room all day. I wasn't as energetic as them, but we shared the love of adventure. So, I knew we wouldn't be sitting in this room as Kagan wanted.

After a lot of convincing and finally putting it to a vote, we ended up swimming in the backyard using the spare clothes we kept in each other's closets. Our parents didn't even care where we slept as long as they knew where we were.

We took turns doing cannonballs, flips, and turns as we dove into the pool. When we got tired of that activity, the twins chased me and tried to dunk my head underwater, but I was a faster swimmer, so they had difficulty catching me, and I ended up tackling them from behind instead. I looked up with a grin and met Godric's eyes, who watched from the lounge chair; he didn't always partake in the fun, but he was entertained in watching us since I saw him break into a faint smile as he watched the twins and me.

Kagan sat rigidly on the other chair, alert and serious—as always—like he was constantly expecting trouble. I could often swear he had cast a protective spell on us since I felt it in the air when he did. It was something I learned to recognize—the subtle energies Vampires used. As we got older, my sensitivity increased to the subtle shifts in my surroundings. I could now read a person's energy clearly—it was like spoken words. Perhaps it was my power, but every Vampire should be able to recognize and read energies. Although, admittedly, I did it better than even an adult Vampire.

I climbed out of the pool and hugged Godric.

"Ser, you're getting me wet," he grumbled.

I flashed him a grin. "Good, now you can join us."

He chuckled and shook his head.

I opened my mouth to convince him, but my words turned into a squeal as Liam carried me firefighter-style. Then he jumped into the pool, followed by Colin pulling my leg as I went under with my mouth open. I broke the water, coughing and sputtering.

Kagan was beside me instantly. He carried me out as I coughed up water. "I'm fine," I said in between more coughs, as I squeezed my eyes shut, and plugged my burning nose. I blinked and saw Godric glaring at the twins, who were approaching. "You two better stay away before I dunk your heads in the water and keep you there for a few minutes," he threatened.

"Are you okay?" Colin asked in concern but didn't step any closer.

"Sorry, Ser." Liam wore a guilty look on his face as he stood next to his brother.

"Guys, I'm fine. Seriously. I just didn't close my mouth fast enough," I said in irritation.

Sometimes the quad were too protective of me—even the twins took my safety seriously, which sometimes ruined our fun. We had argued many times about their overreaction, but they wouldn't budge if they thought there was any danger remotely involved.

The twins were cocky and thought they could protect me, so they were more amiable with having fun, but were also just as stubborn as Godric and Kagan.

After that incident, the four of them wouldn't stop fussing, and the twins refused to play, so we just stood around the pool. It got boring and annoying, so I toweled off and told them I was heading home.

"I'll go with you," Kagan said.

I didn't even bother arguing. Though, I drove here alone. I didn't know why I needed the company.

I got off my moped and hardly looked back from the top of the stairs. "Are you coming in? I think I can make it inside fine on my own."

When I didn't get an answer, I turned to catch him studying me. "What?" I snapped.

He shook his head and jogged up the stairs. We went straight to my room so I could shower.

The setup of our rooms was almost identical, except I had a more feminine decor. We joked around that our parents planned to make us as similar as possible. Except my parents got a girl instead of a boy. It was a surprise we had unique identities. It was like they wanted to make us clones of each other or something. The twins embraced their similarities, but the rest of us tried to differentiate ourselves from one another. Since more often than not, everyone saw us as one unit instead of individuals. It bothered me more than the guys since they were very tight-knit and wouldn't let an outsider in.

When I got out of the bathroom, Kagan was once again in front of a computer. "You know, you don't need to stay with me if you have stuff to do." Not sure what he was so consumed about since it was the summer break before we started high school.

He turned and once again gave me a strange look—something I hadn't seen before. I looked down on what I was wearing; shorts and camisole but saw nothing wrong with it.

"What? Why do you keep looking at me that way?"

"Nothing. Come here." He moved to the couch and tapped the space next to him.

"Okay. Weird much." He had been acting strange all day.

"I'm sorry. I know I've been off all day. I told you, I just had a rough night at practice." He grabbed my hands and played with my fingers.

My brows rose in surprise since Kagan didn't touch me unless he needed to. "Did you want to talk about it?" I studied him closely as my mind raced to horrible things. "Are you okay?"

His golden-brown eyes framed by thick lashes lifted to meet my black ones. "Nothing serious, we're just starting on hard spells. It requires a lot of energy, so it always leaves me exhausted after." He reached up and tucked my wet, black hair behind my ear. Another anomaly about me: both my parents were blond with blue eyes, but I had black-brown hair and eyes. I used to think I was adopted, but I looked so much like both of my parents.

His eyes captured mine and held it until the staring made me uncomfortable. "You know you mean a lot to me. I don't want anything to happen to you, so I won't apologize for wanting to protect you," he said.

I rolled my eyes and leaned away, but then he cupped my face gently and slowly brought our faces closer, until his lips were pressing on mine. *What the hell?*

My eyes grew in shock, and I froze. I didn't know what to think or how to feel. His tongue parted my mouth open as my heart hammered behind my chest. Kagan had his eyes closed while I was still frozen in shock. I felt his tongue caress mine, which made me gasp in a sharp breath at the foreign sensation that had my entire body heating up. He pulled away abruptly.

"I'm so sorry. I..."

I sat frozen for a few more seconds as my mind caught up with unfamiliar emotions. I hadn't thought of the guys in any way aside from my best friends. Nor had I been interested in boys. I was always with the quad, so I hadn't had a chance to really get to know anyone. I'd heard the girls gush about the quad, but I must admit, I hadn't looked at them in any romantic capacity.

"Ser, please say something. I'm sorry. I don't know what came over me. I just...Are you mad?"

I touched my lips, still in shock. I had never kissed a boy before. I never thought it would feel that way. I'd seen people kiss, but didn't see what the fuss was about, but now I know. I finally glanced at him, but he was already up and walking out of the door.

Chapter 2

Kagan

"What did I do? Fuck!" I kept wandering the roads until the buzz in my veins dissipated to a manageable level. *I can't believe I did that.*

I grew up knowing Serris was my mate. However, it was just a word until about fifth or sixth grade. I'd always felt protective of her when we were kids, and I always needed to be near her, but that was it. She was one of my best friends.

One day, Serris teased me about not being affectionate, then she threw herself at me and latched on like a monkey. I was about three inches taller than her, so I caught her easily. Her silky, long, black hair was all over her face. So, I brushed it off, and then I got a whiff of her scent. I stared at her petite features, shiny dark eyes, high cheekbones, small button nose, and thick red lips, and something inside of me stirred. It was the first time I felt our mate bond.

The desire to kiss her was so intense that I dropped her. That was the beginning of my attraction to Serris. It grew more intense with each passing year as I obsessively thought about kissing her, and I often caught myself staring at her.

Seeing another boy look at her or talk to her brought on violent urges in me—sometimes even with the guys. The guys and I kept no secrets from one another, so we talked about our bond with Serris. So, I know we shared the same attraction and the same obsessive desire and possessiveness toward our mate.

We kept watching her for hints to show she felt the same way, but there was nothing. Even Colin and Liam never got hints during the few occasions they became aware of her thoughts and feelings. I would lay awake at night, picturing what it would be like finally kissing her. When it happened, it was everything I had imagined and more.

I didn't know what had come over me. My training with Jarius had been intense as he pushed me more. He'd told me examples of protectors failing to protect their queen, leading to harm or death, and it had rocked me. The thought of any injury to Serris brought me physical pain. It left me anxious and unable to sleep. The feeling had still lingered when she came over; I needed the reassurance that she was fine, and I would not lose her—so I'd kissed her. Which turned out to be a big fucking mistake. *How can something so amazing lead to this? We can't lose her over this.* My entire body tensed at the thought.

I hiked up the mountain behind the compound, the same mountain Serris and the twins got lost in, until I lost track of time. The need to head back had been nagging at me, but I didn't want to face the guys. However, everything inside of me wanted to see Serris again, and the need to inhale her scent and kiss her soft lips left my limbs jittery.

I stopped in front of a fork in the road. I was debating which road to take when I heard a commotion behind me, which made me erect a shield instantly. Godric and the twins appeared, looking murderous. I dropped the shield and placed my hands in my pockets as I braced myself for what they had to say.

The twins glared at me, and Godric wore a blank, cold mask as he said in a hard tone, "You already know that the twins picked up on what happened. My question to you is, why are you here instead of talking to us about it?"

I bowed my head and kicked a pebble on the ground.

"Aren't you going to say anything?" Colin crossed his arms and fixed me a hard stare. "What happened to our agreement? Not to make a move until she shows a hint of what she wants."

"I'm sorry. I fucked up, okay." I looked up to see their expressions hadn't changed. "It just happened." I shrugged.

Godric approached. "You're our leader. You can't be making these kinds of mistakes."

"I know." I sighed and spun to sit on a large boulder. "I didn't plan on it." I looked at them pleadingly. They didn't answer but continued to glare. "What did you...? How is she feeling?" I peered at the twins, bracing for their response.

Liam crossed his arms. "She's confused and shocked."

Colin narrowed his gaze. "Same. She didn't think of us in that way, we're just her friends. Now, she's confused. What does this mean, Kagan? Are we allowed to make a move now?"

I rested my head on my hands. "I don't know. I didn't think it through."

"They warned us not to interfere with her progress. This can mess with that," Godric said in a clipped tone.

"Yeah, plus what happens if she only wants to date you? Or worse, what if she avoids us because of this?" Liam said.

"Are we okay with just one of us dating her?" Colin turned to his brother, who shook his head. Then to Godric, who scowled at the thought.

"Yeah, I don't think it's fair if only one of us gets to date her." I bowed my head. "I'm sorry, I fucked up. What can we do?"

"Take us back to your house so we can discuss this further." Godric looked around with a frown.

The guys and I had the ability to flash to each other's location, but only I could flash us to another place. I was sure eventually, Serris would be able to flash to us, but her powers hadn't manifested yet.

I sat heavily on the single couch while Godric stood, and the twins shared the long sofa. "How are we going to proceed?" Liam asked.

"What if this messes up her progress? Based on what the twins said, she doesn't think of us romantically. Now, she's confused. She also didn't consider dating all of us. The thought confuses and scares her. So that's out of the question. Perhaps she'll be ready to date you, but that's it." Godric glared from behind the couch.

"If you allow that to happen, what if it affects her bond with the rest of us?" Colin leaned forward and fixed me a hard stare.

"I can stay away from her." As I said the words, my stomach filled with dread. *However, I had to fix my mistake so I will do what's needed*. Our bond with her was crucial. Each one of us played a vital role in protecting her. I couldn't jeopardize our primary purpose in protecting her and the Vampire race over my desires. They had raised me to make hard decisions, and this was one of them.

Ever since I was a child, my parents had been training me to be a leader. My practices with Jarius weren't just for magical purposes, but for mental and emotional resiliency. The guys had also been going through the same training. We had to grow up at a very young age. I couldn't really say that we had a childhood, since they had reared us to be warriors from birth.

It was important for Serris to experience a full childhood. We were told from birth of the story of how our parents became councils. The queen, who was connected to all Vampires, sensed when we were conceived. She then brought our parents into the council and others who would play an essential role in Serris' success. She had told our parents the story of her predecessor, who grew up as royalty and didn't experience a normal childhood. She felt a disconnect with the Vampires' lives and had been cruel with no compassion, which led to suppression and disregard for her people. We were told how important it was for Serris to learn the values and lessons of life as an average Vampire before inheriting her full power.

"You know that's not possible. Go ahead and think about not seeing or being close to Serris. Tell me if you can do it?" Liam raised a brow, his tone challenging.

I bowed my head in defeat. "I can't. It's impossible."

"Then what do you recommend?" Colin raised his brows. He had his hands steepled under his chin.

I didn't want to suggest it, but it was the only solution I could think of. I had been racking my brain for answers, but it was the only thing that made sense. Releasing a pent-up breath, I pushed up and paced.

"You can't be serious?" Colin stood facing me.

Fuck! He must have read my mind. He could only pick up our thoughts when we were emotional. The queen's protectors taught us to block the twins' power, but they warned us it would fail when we were at a heightened emotion. It was like a fail-safe built-in for our protection.

"What? What is he thinking?" Liam's gaze bounced from Colin and me.

Colin's nose flared. "He wants all of us to stay away from her."

"What?"

"You can't be serious?"

"It's the only thing that makes sense. We can't rush her progress, and we can't risk our bond," I implored.

"I thought we already established that it's literally impossible not to be near her. That's why our parents made the arrangements they did and why they encouraged our closeness." Godric braced his hands on the back of the couch with a look of controlled patience. He looked intimidating, but I didn't back down. *I needed to fix my mistake.*

"I know that!" I snapped. "I meant, we tell her we can't see her anymore, and we still watch over her without her knowing."

"You're fucking crazy," Liam said.

"Fuck that," Colin said.

Godric's eyes narrowed, but he kept quiet.

"Do any of you have any ideas? It's the best I have. Like you pointed out, we can't risk her bonding with just one of us, and we can't rush her progress."

"Why can't we just see how it goes and then act?" Godric asked.

"Wouldn't it be harder to break it off if we allow it to continue? You know her. Once she decides, that's it. She's stubborn as hell. If she comes to me, I don't think I can deny her. Did you want to risk that?"

"You fucking did this. Now we all have to pay for your mistakes." Liam stood next to Colin as they wore an identical scowl.

"I'm sorry. How many times do I have to say it? I made a mistake."

"Yes. A mistake with great consequences that affects all of us," Godric hissed.

The statement felt worse than a punch. *I knew he was right.* "You can't be making these mistakes as a leader." He held my eyes for a moment and walked out the door.

The twins glowered at me for a moment longer, then followed Godric out. I dropped to the couch and prepared myself to break Serris' heart. It would kill me to do it, but it was necessary. The guys would hate me for it, but they knew it was the right thing to do. They were right, though. I couldn't let my emotions rule my actions since there was too much at stake.

Serris

I couldn't sleep. I kept thinking about Kagan's kiss, which filled me with confusion. It was like his lips triggered these emotions inside of me. Something I didn't know existed. I thought about how affectionate the guys were toward me, and now I didn't know if that meant something other than years of friendship. Then cold washed over me. *What if this ruins our friendship?* I shook it off as the thought of not being able to touch them or hang out with them brought pain in me. However, I couldn't stop my brain from thinking romantic thoughts.

The thought of kissing Kagan, with his angled jaw and intense golden eyes, brought butterflies in my stomach. I could also envision the twins who had glacier blue eyes and dark hair, with deep dimples that come out when they smiled. Godric's bulky muscles were sexy as hell mixed with his soft feminine features made him look like an avenging angel.

The thought of kissing all four had me excited but at the same time scared. I had been so confused with my new feelings that I stayed up most of the night, trying to figure out what it had all meant. It wasn't possible to like all four of them. I definitely didn't want to lose their friendship by complicating our relationship, so I had to ignore these new feelings I had.

I woke up the next day, filled with nervous anxiety. As I got ready, I took extra care of how I looked—something I hadn't cared about in the past since they had seen me at my worst while we were growing up together—and no one cared.

I wanted to feel attractive and feminine. I wanted them to see me as a girl.

My heart raced when I met up with them at the twins' house, whose parents were away.

I tucked my blow-dried hair behind my ears as I approached the boys in the living room and smiled nervously. "Hi, guys." I glanced at Kagan, but he avoided my eyes.

The twins didn't jump up and try to tackle me, so I knew something was wrong—plus the room was filled with serious energy. I sat at the far end of the sofa, giving me enough distance from the quad, who had their backs straight, shoulders tense, and their hands clenched.

I didn't want to ask as fear twisted in my stomach, so I kept my head bowed. "What's going on?" I whispered and peeked at them from under my lashes.

The twins glared at Kagan, while Godric crossed his arms with a clenched jaw. His dark energy was swirling around him.

My palms broke out in sweat, and dread filled me. "Someone talk soon, or I'm leaving. I don't like the energy you're throwing my way."

"We need to talk, Serris," Kagan started, which made me wary since he only called me by my full name when he was angry or emotional.

"Okay, talk." I crossed my arms and frowned.

"I...We..." Liam snorted, and Kagan glared at him. "We think it's best not to hang out as much anymore."

My face flooded with heat, and I shot up from my seat with balled fists. "Is this because of what happened yesterday?" I sucked in air through my nose and let it out noisily as I tried to control my anger. I opened my mouth to speak a few times, but words wouldn't come out. "Because I didn't ask for it."

They blasted me with jumbled emotions of pain, anger, and jealousy. I absorbed their energy and read more into their feelings than what they had failed to convey with their words. *I can't believe it, they were dumping me just because of one kiss.* My heart contracted in pain as I fisted my shaking hands and glared at all of them, while fighting hard against the negative energy they were throwing around the room. "Are you all agreeing to this?" My voice shook as I swallowed a lump in my throat. "You want to throw away our lifelong friendship because of one stupid kiss?" I demanded, but they didn't meet my eyes.

The anger surging from them had my knees buckling. Godric pushed off his chair, and began pacing behind the couch, but he refused to meet my eyes and didn't say a word.

My heart broke then. If someone was going to put a stop to this, it was Godric. If he agreed to this plan, then there was nothing I could do to change their minds. Betrayal hit me. It was more robust than whatever energy they were throwing my way. My heart cracked, and I gasped in pain as I tried to contain the tears. I braced myself on the arm of the chair as my world crashed down on me. *How could they do this to me? My best friends. How could they throw away a lifelong friendship over one stupid kiss? How can they treat me this way?*

The twins moved to get up and took a step toward me, then stopped. Godric froze in place as he watched but didn't make a move. Kagan wore a blank expression, his posture rigid.

It was ironic. Just yesterday, their overprotectiveness had annoyed me, and here I was longing for them to come and rush to my side and comfort me. *Pathetic.*

I moved to leave, but then they all took a step toward me, talking all at once.

"Ser..."

"Let us explain."

"Wait."

I lifted my palm out and said, "Stop!" They all paused mid-movement. I was uncertain what made them stop, but they looked frozen in place. Uncaring, I ran out of the house in tears.

I stayed in my room for days, crying my eyes out. My parents heard about what happened, and I hoped they would intervene, but they took the guys' side. "Perhaps it's for the best," they said, which was another blow of betrayal. *My own parents. Why was this happening?*

I lay wide awake for several nights, overthinking every moment and trying to decipher what had happened since I still couldn't believe they could throw away our lifelong friendship easily. *There had to be more to it.*

For weeks I would wake up with renewed hope that one of them would change their minds. Then each day ended with fresh heartbreak. After a while, hope left me, and I was left with misery and loneliness.

I could have sworn I even felt the twins in my room a few times, but then I would wake up, and they weren't there. *It was my lowest.* I missed them so much that I was hallucinating they were around me.

I tried texting them a few times, asking if they were over their craziness, but I got no response. One day I was so furious and hurt that I blew up their phones with phone calls and messages, but I still got no answer. After almost a month, I was determined to get one of them to talk. I went to each of their houses, but they refused to see me. Their parents said the same thing as mine. *Perhaps it was for the best.*

My anger built as I counted down the end of summer. By the time the first day of high school approached. I was beyond hurt and in full rage. I walked the halls, determined to give them a piece of my mind or make them suffer as much as they made me. In my haste to find the quad, I overlooked Irina until I bumped into her. Her parents belong to the council, so I've hung out with her a few times.

"Watch it!" She snapped.

With a brow and a hard stare, I said, "*You* watch it." I waited for her to say something else, but she didn't. I was itching to lash out at anyone at this point. Irina, who was mean to everyone, studied me for a moment, and then her lips quirked up. "A new and feisty Serris. I like it."

I shook my head and moved to step away, but she followed me. "What do you want?" I asked.

"Who are you after? I can help. I know that look."

I brushed her off with a bump of a shoulder. "None of your business. Go away."

"I'm really liking this new you. Plus, you're not surrounded by your bodyguards. You are showing BFF material."

"Not interested." I threw my books in the locker and slammed it shut as I glared at anyone who dared to look my way.

"I fucking love this new you. You're bitchier than me," she said with glee. Then she followed me around all morning and wouldn't leave me alone.

By lunchtime, I had better control of my anger. However, I still had a bitchy attitude. Ciaran and Kier, whose parents were in the council, joined Irina and I at our table. They rarely joined the quad and me, but the council family members typically stuck together. Our lifestyle was too different from the rest of the kids in school that it was easier to lean on each other.

Kier had always flirted with me, but I just brushed it off as his playboy personality. We all grew up together, but they didn't want to be around the quad because the douchebags didn't welcome anyone into their web. I thought I was part of their group, but I was sorely mistaken, given how easily they dumped me. My face flamed with anger and embarrassment as my thoughts turned dark. I didn't notice how hard I was gripping my sandwich.

Kier pried it out of my hands and said, "Easy there. It didn't do anything to you." He took my hands and gently wiped off the remnants of my wasted lunch. I looked up, but he was looking at me the same way Kagan looked at me the night he'd kissed me. My face flamed, and a new kind of heat replaced my anger. I looked away in embarrassment, but not before I caught the slight smile on Kier's face.

"Oh, look. Are you all suddenly friends now?" Kagan said in an obnoxious drawl.

I stiffened up as I heard his voice behind me. "Why the fuck do you care? Go mind your own goddamn business." I glared. *He had some fucking nerve.*

Kier placed a comforting hand on my back, and I noticed Godric's eyes narrow at his hand.

"No worries, we're not interested in any of your business. You are all insignificant," Kagan said as he looked at each of us in disdain.

I laughed mockingly. "Yet, you decided to make your way towards us? What's wrong, Kagan? Are you losing your touch? Why don't you run along now and give us some privacy?" I scooted closer to Kier and looked up at him from under my lashes. He flashed me a big grin and faced the guys with a sneer.

I noticed the veins in Kagan's neck pop as he clenched his jaw. Godric looked like he was minutes from losing it. The twins had their heads bowed and wouldn't meet my eyes.

"Run along now. It looks like one of you is about to lose control. You wouldn't want that, would you?" I flashed them a sweet smile and dismissed them entirely.

"Girl. What the hell happened?" Ciaran asked once the quads were out of earshot.

"Oh, we are definitely jamming this year," Irina said.

Once I was certain the quad had left the cafeteria, I turned to Kier and said, "I'm sorry, I didn't mean to use you like that."

"Serris, you can use me anytime." He winked.

I blushed and let out a chuckle as I ignored the looks we were getting from everyone. I was sure by the end of the day, everyone would be talking about my breakup with the quad.

Chapter 3
Serris

It had been almost four years since the quad stopped being friends with me. We went from lifelong friends to enemies. In the beginning, their harsh words were like lashes to my heart as I had never realized that I had romantic feelings towards them. Losing their company left a gaping hole in my heart, which made it hard to breathe, but I had learned to start over and live without them.

Now, the only feeling I had of the quad was anger. They had become my mortal enemies since they'd sabotaged anything good in my life for the past four years.

After the boys in school realized the quad and I were done for good, they started paying me some attention. However, each time the quad would catch me with a guy, they would say something horrible toward us. The few guys who had shown interest in me eventually gave up, or worse, stood me up when we'd make plans for a date.

I suffered from severe insecurity—the quad's words would echo in my head. *Serris, you don't really believe he likes you for you, do you? He just wants the prestige of dating a council's daughter. Or he only wants our second-hand discard. You don't even have an active power.* It wasn't just words; I truly believed that no one liked me. Afterall, the quad dropped me after a lousy kiss.

In my junior year, Irina and I had done our own investigation with Ciaran's help. We found out that the quad had been bullying my dates behind my back and would even go as far as threatening harm to them if they continued to pursue me. One time, Godric had given one of them a bloody nose. My all-time favorite was threatening their families with the power of the council. We'd also discovered that they had been successful in sabotaging my party life. We simply thought we were unlucky because something unfortunate would happen when I plan to attend a party. From my parents finding out or the host parents canceling the party. Either way, the A-holes had achieved their goal because I had a lifetime ban from parties—my parents forbade me from going out past dark.

I suspected the quad had something to do with my parents' sudden strictness. They seemed to support whatever the quad did. I once hinted that they had been bullying me, and as usual, they either turned a deaf ear, or they'd say it was for the best. Since then, I had surmised the entire council was on the quad's side.

Perhaps it was because they were powerful; they had so much pull toward the council and at school. Even Ciaran and Irina reported the same results from their parents when they told them what was happening. The quad was basically untouchable.

I'd been lucky to have Irina in my life. She had stuck by me and had been a fierce friend in the last few years. She, Ciaran, and I had been inseparable.

Now a senior, I planned to enjoy the last year of school. I was determined to finally beat the quad at their own game.

"We're on for Saturday," Irina whispered. We weren't taking any chances that the quad or some spies with supernatural hearing were listening in on our plans. Irina was throwing me a party for my eighteenth birthday. Of course, it wasn't on my actual birthday because that would have been too risky. She and Ciaran were throwing a random party and pretending I wouldn't be going as always. It would be easy since everyone knew I wasn't allowed to attend parties.

"Hey, beautiful," Kier said as he sat at our table. I smiled as we held each other's gaze for a moment. My face flushed, and I hid behind my soda can as I gulped it down loudly.

He and I had been talking for several months now. He had been trying to get with me for the past few years, but it was never a good time. He had since toned down his playboy ways. We snuck and planned our dates right under the quad's noses and had secretly gone out a few times and even shared a kiss a few times.

He said his parents had been curious and had been asking who he was dating, but he hadn't told them anything. Irina and Ciaran had helped us by keeping tabs on the quad and giving us the go signal. *I'm so lucky to have them as friends*. Irina was still bitchy to others, but she had been a loyal friend.

I gazed at my two best friends when a full soda bottle hit Kier's head. I looked up and saw Colin flash his evil grin. "My bad. I had meant to throw that to my brother."

I heard a chuckle behind me and saw Liam wearing an identical grin.

Kier stood up, radiating anger as the twins dropped their faked smiles and stood straight, casting violence toward Kier. In the past four years, the twins had shot up and towered over everyone at slightly over six feet tall. With swimmers' bodies and intense eyes, the two of them are the most beautiful creatures I've laid eyes on—precisely how the ancient text described Vampires. Before humans knew about supernaturals, they wrote novels about Vampires, and it always described them as beautiful creatures. Too bad the twins were rotten to the core, and I had to suffer through their tricks throughout the years; now, all I saw when I looked at them was a pretty rose filled with thorns. Their faces were weapons they used right before they struck.

"What are you going to do about it, lover boy?" Colin sneered, using his Vampire speed to stand next to his brother. When Vampires used their powers, it was always to show superiority.

Heat flooded in me as I got up. I wasn't taking their shit this year. *I had been too nice in the past and let things go with just a few words but, I'm done playing nice.* I'd spent enough years in misery because of them, and I was ready to throw down with them. My nose flared, and I clenched my fists tightly as I stood next to Kier.

I really liked Kier, and the quad would not drive him away. I felt my anger rise and as the moment passed, I could see it radiate off me in waves.

My power had grown. I could now read everyone's energy for miles. Not only could I read them, but I could also manipulate them if I wanted to. No one knew, not even my parents, because they were not on my side, but I suspected with the right training; I could do much more with it. Instead, I had been practicing on my own. At first, I could only read one person's emotions; eventually, I could wield them to do my bidding. When I had potent emotions, I could permeate my surroundings with the same feeling and infect others to feel as I felt. Recently, I had been training to use my energy to move things.

"Back the fuck off," I said in a low voice. As I stood before the twins, I could see the potent, angry energy coming off me and seep into the entire room. I knew from the worried glances the twins shared that they were reading the kids' minds and emotions in the cafeteria. I bet the whole room was directing the same amount of anger I had toward them.

They glanced at me in surprise, as hurt flashed in their eyes before turning away without another word.

"What the hell was that?" Irina asked.

Ciaran rushed me out of the room and into the grounds, while Irina and Kier were hot on our heels.

"What? Why are you two acting weird?" I pulled to a stop when we were far away from anyone to hear.

Ciaran waved his hand and used his caster powers to enclose us in a bubble to make our conversation private.

"Were you not aware of what you just did?" Irina had her hands on her hips with her brows furrowed.

Ciaran wore the same expression.

"What do you mean?"

"You manipulated everyone's feelings in there. We were ready to rip the twins apart if you willed us to," Irina said.

I chuckled because Irina liked to exaggerate.

"She's not joking, Ser," Kier said.

"I thought you didn't have an active power?" Ciaran asked.

"I don't. I mean...I might have experienced a few outbursts now and then, but nothing to show a talent. I've always been able to read emotions and do something with it, but that's it." I shrugged.

"Well, that was one hell of a talent. You literally infected the whole cafeteria. I don't know how far your influence goes, but that was scary to witness." Kier tucked his hands inside his jeans pockets and flashed me a worried look. *Wow, I knew I could infect others with my feelings, but I didn't realize I could make them attack my enemies.*

I glanced at Kier. He was adorable. He wasn't as tall as the quad; he was shy of six feet with a lean body, green eyes, and dirty-blond hair that he liked to keep long on one side and shaved on the other and he had a cute chin dimple.

"We need to figure out your powers before you give yourself away like that again. I don't think people know it came from you." Irina had one arm crossed while the other rested on top as she tapped on her lip with her forefinger.

"Yeah, that's probably a good idea. Did I ever say, I'm so lucky to have you guys?" Irina and Ciaran wrapped their arms around me as Kier flashed me a sweet smile.

"We should go, or we'll be late." Ciaran tugged on my hand.

Kier waved goodbye, and then Irina walked into the class next to ours. Ciaran and I have fourth period together, which we walked into just as Mr. Destry, a Fae who teaches advanced history, entered. He started his lecture right away, so it was best not to be late for his class.

"Okay, everyone. We are done summarizing what you should have learned in the past three years, so now I would like to start a new section. In the past, you have learned the intricate details about the war that caused the liberation of supernaturals. Now it's time for us to go into the microscopic view. This part is important to see how such a significant history affected our very being. Can someone tell me the reason the war started?"

He looked around, but no one raised their hands, even though it was common knowledge. "Eric?" He called on one of the few humans in Atrus High School, which was located right on the outskirts of Abrea. The rulers had standardized our education to allow all races to mingle and encouraged all races to live together in territories. Our school had a few humans, Casters, and some Fae—however, no Werewolves since they were our natural enemies. Although we lived in peaceful existence with them, it didn't mean we were ready to integrate.

"The Dark Seelie King wanted to rule all races, so he exposed the existence of supernaturals to humans." Eric's ears turned red as he spoke and kept his gaze on his desk. He was super friendly and always smiled when you passed him in the halls.

"That's correct. This started the war between humans and supernaturals. Even though humans were powerless back then, they had numbers and technology. They fought back by hunting all supernaturals and showed no mercy, which started several years of conflict between the races. The wolves protected humans as it was in their nature to do so. The Vampires weren't involved much since their ancestors were mindless beasts." Mr. Destry paused as he clicked on the slide that showed graphic pictures of the ancient war.

"The Fae divided between Seelie and Unseelie. The Seelie knows that if earth perished, so will Faerie, so they protected the humans. After years of fighting, some humans eventually recognized the supernaturals who protected them. It started with only a handful of humans, then a lot of them changed their attitude towards supernaturals. Some underground groups formed and advocated for a change of policies in how supernaturals were treated. A secret supernatural group also emerged. Once they had some important human ears, they brought the proposal to each race's leader. It was how the Rulers Consortium was formed. They brought on a new era in what we know as the new world."

He looked around and asked, "Can anyone tell me who all on the Consortium are?"

A Fae girl raised her hand. She and a few of them were new transfers who keep to themselves. "There were five kingdoms at first. Lasite for the Seelie, Roudal for the Shifters, Neutera for humans, Crelan for Vampires, and Lavania for Casters. Eventually, after the years of fighting had stopped, the Vivid kingdom of the Unseelie joined."

"That's correct. Each kingdom divided the seven continents. Some took whole continents, while the Fae claimed the forests, and they divided big cities between Vampires and humans. Casters also preferred to be with nature, so they took what was not owned by the Fae or mountains that Shifters did not occupy. The humans claimed more land since they surpass any race in numbers." He looked up as the bell rang. "Okay, we will touch on how those events affected each race next time."

Irina, Ciaran, and I met up and carpooled back to the compound. We picked each other up every morning. Then after school, we mostly spent our time at Irina's place since her parents were hardly home, so it was safer talking there than at our house.

"So, we have everything planned out for Saturday. Bret and I will pretend to go out on a date, and while we do that, we will keep an eye out on the quad. Ciaran and Kristo will be our backup. Everything is taken care of, so all we have to do is show up," Irina said in between bites of chips.

Ciaran grabbed a handful of chips and stuffed it all in his mouth.

"Geez, Ciar, hungry much?" Irina said with a raised brow.

"Bitch, don't call me that. I hate that name. It sounds so masculine. I prefer my given name."

"Bitch, you're such a diva. Why are you eating like you haven't eaten in days?" Irina slowly dragged the bag of chips away from him.

"I've been on a diet for a week, and now I'm off so I can eat whatever I want."

My brows furrowed. "Isn't that a human thing? Vampires don't get fat, so there is no need for us to diet. Our metabolism is too fast."

He shrugged as he glared at Irina, who hid the chips from him. "Girl, I will eat you if you don't feed me."

I busted out laughing. "For God's sake, feed the caveman."

"I am no caveman," he said with a stuffed mouth.

Irina and I glanced at each other and laughed.

"Okay, I know it was stupid. I just thought it would make my skin glow if I ate healthier. So, I cut all the junk in my diet."

"Your skin will glow if you consume the right amount of supplements," I said.

"How would I know if I were consuming enough?"

"Listen to your body. If you start craving iron or raw steak, then you're not consuming enough. If your speed and strength is down, then you're consuming too much," Irina said, handing him a bag of carrots.

He scrunched his face and grudgingly took one. He popped a few more and said, "These shits are actually good. Are they special carrots or something?"

"No, they're just baby carrots."

"Sweet and crunchy. I love it."

"Seriously, Ciaran. What's going on? Why are you tripping?" I asked as I reached for a carrot.

"Kristo and I have been talking, and we might be ready to take our relationship to the next level." He glanced at us hesitantly.

"So, what does that have to do with your diet and glowing skin?" Irina asked with a confused look.

"I wanted to look good. I know it sounds stupid, but it's our first time, so I wanted it to be perfect."

"Like the first time ever or first time together?" I asked.

"Or the more appropriate question, is this your first with a guy?" Irina walked out of the kitchen, and Ciaran and I followed her. He still clutched his bag of carrots as I carried our sodas. We walked up to her room, where we usually gossiped and did some homework.

"It's the first for both of us ever," he said dramatically as he lay on Irina's bed.

"Really? I would have never thought that about Kristo."

"Well, he's been in the closet up until last year. That was when we started talking."

"Exactly. Are you sure he hasn't been with a girl?" Irina raised a brow.

He placed his hand on his forehead. "Ugh, you two aren't helping my anxiety. I'm sure because he told me. Yes, he dated to see if he liked girls, but he felt a sense of wrongness when they started making out. So, nothing happened." He smirked.

"Interesting. I would never have guessed," Irina said.

"What about you and Bret?" I asked.

"What about us? We are experienced lovers and continue to pleasure each other every chance we get."

"Geez, it's called too much information." Ciaran covered his ears and screwed up his face.

I laughed at the two.

"We're not even going to ask about Kier, but are you finally going to go for it?" Ciaran raised a brow.

"Maybe. I really like him. I just haven't thought about it."

"Well, it's because you don't know what you're missing. Don't overthink it, just go for it," Irina said.

"You think so?" I asked as I played at the fringe of the pillow on my lap.

"Yes. If the moment feels right, then go for it. The only reason Kris and I had been taking it slow and overly planning this is because we're not actually completely out in the open. Otherwise, we would have done it a long time ago."

"We'll see." I shrugged nonchalantly, but deep inside, I felt excitement and a pang of intense guilt. I'm not sure why I would feel guilty. I'm not with anyone.

The nagging feeling stayed with me throughout the night, but I figured it was just nervousness. I hadn't been with a boy romantically except for a few stolen kisses with Kier, but it didn't count because it left me wanting more. My only other experience was the kiss with Kagan, which ended in a disaster, so it was time for me to experience life.

Chapter 4
Serris

On Friday, Ciaran and I made it to our last class early, eager for school to be over since we had some planning to do after school.

"Okay, class. Where were we?" He flipped pages on his book and then continued as he walked in front of the board. "Yes, we ended with the division of land. After they formed the Rulers Consortium, changes had been swift. They passed laws that made it illegal to hunt down another race without cause and soon started promoting integration." He walked back to his desk and started his projector. "We will finish up this section by learning how the war affected each race down to their DNA. With supernaturals out in the open and working with humans, it brought an era of rapid growth in science and technology. New innovations from combining supernatural knowledge with humans allowed each race to progress to a more developed society." A picture of a rabid Vampire with red eyes and blood dripping on his fangs showed on the image. "Of course, it took centuries to see noticeable changes. For example, with humans' help, Vampires successfully isolated the gene that made them crave blood. Then they developed blood replacements. It took years, but eventually, most Vampires opted to drink the replacement and lived civilly amongst others. After centuries of not drinking blood, the Vampire's DNA changed to what we see today. Vampires no longer crave blood but still need to take supplements to ensure they do not deprive their bodies of the required nutrients to survive." He kept clicking and showed Vampires looking more and more human. Our ancestors had unearthly beauty; only a few of us looked like them. I squirmed in my seat as I realized I looked like my ancestors with my pale skin, red lips, and black hair, except I didn't have the red eyes. The twins had similar beauty, except they were blond, and their eyes were unnaturally blue.

"With these changes in DNA, Vampires are now born, not made. They also developed extra abilities their ancestors didn't have. There are several theories on how this happened. The most plausible one is that, with the changes in Vampire DNA, your bodies are now"—he held up air quotes—"alive, and since all supernaturals came from the Fae, the gene is now active. They believe the activated Fae gene is the reason for your extra powers."

Claudia, a Fae, raised her hand.

Mr. Destry paused and raised a brow. "Yes, dear?"

"I have a question. What do you mean all supernaturals came from Fae? Are they Fae with altered genes?"

"No, their genes were not altered. It's believed Vampires are part human, Seelie and Unseelie. While Werewolves are half Unseelie and half human, Casters were made from Seelie and humans."

"Humans aren't from Fae?"

"No. Humans are just humans. The Faerie and the human realm are intertwined. There are portions of Faerie here, which is believed to be essential to sustain the land in Faerie. So back to my story; Vampires were changed, and next were humans. Once the species started mingling, there were more and more interspecies breeding between humans and sups. After centuries of inbreeding, there are very few pure humans left. After all, every race was severely depleted because of the war. Humans got stronger from training their young to fight supernaturals, but that's not all."

He paused and wore a mysterious smile. "The most admirable quality of humans' new generations is their ability inherited from their mixed breeding. No one knows what powers humans have. Of course, they are also very skilled in killing different supernatural breeds, and they are always armed with magical objects. Modern humans had gotten stronger, faster, and their senses had improved as well. Although they are not as fast or as strong as regular sup, they make up for it with their deadly training and spelled weapons. Never again will the humans perish in large numbers." He paused dramatically and looked around as Eric sat straight and with pride. I eyed his necklace that had a blue stone and his belt that hung different weapons and amulets. I could feel the power he carried; he definitely could hold his own in a fight.

"The Fae, Casters, and Werewolves showed some changes but not much. Although, these races like to keep to themselves, so we would never know for sure. What we could confirm is that each race could now mate with humans. Perhaps it's because of human interbreeding, or it could be the cause of something entirely different. Wolves can now control their shift, which means the full moon doesn't drive them as it did with their ancestors. This also means they can partially shift. They too activated their Fae gene and develop extra abilities. While Casters can now do the magic they were not capable of in the past, and they are no longer limited to magical objects or trinkets. Some don't even have to say a spell. They can now rival the Fae in magical abilities. Now, with the Fae, they had reported no changes aside from mating with humans. We are the oldest supernaturals, after all." He leaned on his desk and checked the time on his watch. "With these changes, all creatures on Earth and in Faery are pretty much on an even playing field, so no one would dare try to start another war. They know it wouldn't be as easy as last time." He stood up straight and said, "We will go over more details of past rulers of different races, and we will have a test about the unit by the end of the month." We groaned at his announcement and gathered our things as the bell rang.

Ciaran and I hung out at his house since Irina was out with Bret.

"Are you sure you want to hang out with me tonight? You can go call Kristo, you know. I can go home."

"Nah. He's busy doing family stuff."

"Well, what else do we need to organize for tomorrow?" I asked.

"Do you have an alibi for tomorrow?"

"No need, my parents won't be home. They trust that I won't leave, so I'll just sneak out."

"What if someone is watching your house?"

"Don't worry. I want to be there, so I'll be careful and go through the woods."

"Is that safe? You alone in the woods at night." He frowned.

"I'm a Vampire. What am I supposed to fear at night?"

"Didn't you tell me about the story of when you got lost in the woods and were really scared?"

"Pshh, I was young and stupid then. With no extra abilities, I had plenty of spare time, so my parents had me doing physical training along with weapons training."

"I heard about that. That sounds badass. I wish I knew how to fight."

"You don't need to. You can just throw magic at your opponents."

"Well, yeah, but it's still cool." He picked up his phone as it dinged and scrolled through the messages. "OMG, Kristo just texted. He wants to come over." He jumped in place, looking both excited and terrified at the same time. "What should I do?"

I grabbed both of his hands. "Ciaran, don't overthink it. If the moment is right, it will happen. Now go buff and pluck and get gorgeous before he gets here. I'll show myself out."

He hugged me. "Oh my god, I'm shaking. Look at my hands." He held out his hand, palm down, and I could see it visibly tremble.

I kissed his cheek. "You got this."

"Are you sure you'll be okay to walk home alone?"

"Didn't I just tell you I can kick ass now? Plus, we're inside the compound. What could possibly happen?"

"You're right. Text me when you get home."

"I will. Call me tomorrow." I winked and left.

The night air was cold and pleasant, so I took my time and walked through the park. I didn't want to go home yet, so passing through the park would allow me to enjoy the night. It was rare for me to be alone outside, since I was usually always surrounded by friends or family.

I looked up at the clear sky and took a deep breath. I loved and enjoyed the peace it brought as I walked by myself. It allowed me to think and have a break from sensing others. My powers had been getting stronger and being around people meant I got bombarded with their energies, so sometimes it was hard to shut it out. Even when I was alone, I could still feel them, but it was more muted.

I took the path by the lake and stood for a minute, enjoying the moon cresting the still waters. Twisting at a noise behind me, I allowed my senses to wander but felt nothing. Perhaps it was just some animal, so I started walking again, but this time I heard the definite rustle of someone stepping on dry leaves. I didn't stop walking. Instead, I let my energy sense out who was following me. They were too far away so my Vampire vision and sense of smell couldn't pick them up, but my energy had a limitless range—I could read any energy I directed it to.

I tilted my head and slowed my walk. *What is that?* He must have been masking his energy because I couldn't get a definite read on him. I just knew it was a male, and he was at the entrance of the path I took. *Why is he masking his energy? Is he following me?*

There were a couple of options. I could run and use my Vampire speed to hunt him down or cut through the trees to grab him from behind. I was at the end of the lake, and if I ran fast enough, I could run the perimeter of the lake and sneak behind him before he even realized I was gone.

I wanted to find out who was tracking me, so I ran as fast as I could and snuck in behind him. I hid behind a large tree, making sure not to make a sound until I found my breath. My heart was pounding, but I was sure he wasn't paying attention.

The guy was tall and nicely built, and he wore a hoodie and jeans. He jogged closer to where he would have thought I should be and paused, smelling the air. *The fucker was scenting me*. Before he even had the chance to pinpoint my location, I sped up and used my Vampire strength to leap a few hundred feet and tackled him. With my adrenaline pumping, it enhanced my senses. I pinned his hands to his back and put all of my weight on him as we landed. He was face down with my knee on his neck and I had a good grip on both his hands as I pulled on them at an uncomfortable angle. He grunted and turned his face, which I recognized as Kagan, so I leaped off him instantly. "You! Why the fuck are you following me?"

He rubbed his face and rotated his arms as he grimaced in pain. "Who said I was following you? I was just enjoying the night, and you attacked me."

"Nice fucking try. I've sensed you for a while now."

His eyes grew in surprise by my statement, but I continued before he could say another word. "So, are you going to tell me, or are you gonna keep lying?"

He raised his brow in a cocky way and smirked. "You would like it if I were following you. Wouldn't you? Is that what you fantasize about? That I secretly follow you around?"

My eyes narrowed. *Kagan was pissing me off.* Not because of his shitty attitude, but because he and his creepy friends were always on my business. I stepped closer. My fists clenched to control my anger. When I was toe to toe with him, I leaned in close and said in a low and threatening voice, "I am sick and tired of you four freaks always meddling in my business. This is your only warning. You four back the fuck off, or I won't be responsible for my next actions."

I heard him suck in a breath, and for a moment, I saw the worry in his eyes. Then, just as quickly, his cocky smile was back. "What are you going to do, Ser? You don't have any powers."

It was my turn to smile as I engulfed him with my energy that was swirling with anger. I saw him flinch and his jaw clenched as his face contorted in discomfort. "Last warning, I'm done playing nice. Back the fuck off," I intoned, then stepped away. I used my Vampire speed to run back home.

Liam

We flashed to Kagan's location when we felt his distress. Our bond had gotten stronger, so regardless of the distance, we could locate one another and flash to the other's location during distress. We were also now able to communicate with each other telepathically.

We felt Kagan's pain and tried to contact him, but he didn't respond, so we flashed to him. When we saw Serris, Godric was quick to cloak us in darkness so she wouldn't see us. With Godric's talent of manipulating dark energy, he could cloak us from sight and scent as well. I doubted it cloaked our energy. Ser was too busy on Kagan to sense us. Otherwise, she would have turned on us as well.

"Are you okay?" Colin placed a hand on Kagan's shoulder, but he didn't move. He continued to gaze at the direction Ser disappeared to. He looked pale and had a faraway look on his face.

"Get us out of here, Kagan." I placed a hand on his other arm to get his attention.

He didn't speak; he only looked down and took a deep, stuttered breath then continued to gaze in the direction Ser went. "Godric has her covered." I stepped in front of him, directly in his eye line.

He nodded without bothering to look at us, and we flashed to his bedroom.

He sat down heavily on the couch. "Did you hear?" He looked up from the sofa.

57

He was still emanating shock and worry; it was like he was screaming them at me. I eyed my brother, and he gave me a look that said he was also screaming the same thoughts.

"Yes, we heard and saw everything." Colin sighed next to him.

"Her powers are getting stronger," Kagan whispered. "Why didn't we know about this? We had her covered twenty-four-seven. Not once did it seem like the transfer of powers had begun."

"Are you even surprised? It's Ser." Colin chuckled.

"That's not the worst part. Do you remember what we told you about the incident at lunch?" I crossed my arms.

He nodded.

"She had the same emotions tonight. She meant what she said. If we push her, she won't hold back." My brows drew together as I eyed them both.

"We need a new approach," Colin said in a forceful tone as he clenched and unclenched his jaw.

"She hates us. We've pushed her too far." The words caused a sharp pain in my chest and I could feel that the other two shared my pain. While we had not spoken with her in the last four years, we have closely monitored her. We had been so consumed with keeping her safe and making sure we were on the right track that we pushed her away in the process. I paced restlessly and muttered, "I didn't think she would hate us. How can she hate us? We're her mates." I looked up at a loss. I didn't care that they saw the vulnerability in my eyes or hear the crack in my voice. *Ser is our mate, and we can't lose her.*

"What if she rejects us? Can she do that?" Colin jumped up, his entire body tense as he clenched and unclenched his fist.

He did this when he needed to release some of the tension he was feeling.

Kagan's head snapped to Colin. "Is that possible?"

"How the fuck should I know? Shouldn't you know this? Being our leader and all?" Colin glared at Kagan.

I stopped my pacing. "Let's not fight, guys." We had been lost without Ser. Sometimes, I didn't think we were even friends anymore. In our determination to protect her and focus on success, we four stopped being friends—we didn't talk or have fun together anymore. It hadn't been the same since we cut her out. Now, all we do is argue.

"Well, all I know is she fucking hates us," Colin bit out.

Kagan studied Colin for a moment, then turned to me. "What did she feel?"

"We don't get a read on her often—it's been a while, only when she is angry at us. The last few interactions she had with us...she felt hate." I whispered the last part. It was hard to voice out loud since admitting that your mate hated you didn't feel right. *I refuse to accept it.* The thought of losing our mate, our reason for existing, was even more unfathomable. Our entire world had revolved around her for as long as I could remember. We grew up knowing she was our mate and our queen to protect. We had been training since we were kids for our role and we gave up our childhood because we knew it was our responsibility to protect the queen, and the weight of the Vampire race rested upon us. But neither one of us ever questioned our role or complained because the price was her.

The past four years had been a mind fuck, but we didn't have any other choice. We did it because it was necessary. It wasn't pleasant, but it was what they trained us to do. Make the tough choices. We just didn't think it would come to this.

Kagan ran his hands down his face. I flinched as the pain in my chest doubled—it was his pain and Colin's. We all felt it; *the rejection of our mate was excruciating, and it was our fault.*

"What do we do?" Kagan looked at us with pleading eyes. Kagan—our leader, someone who always had his chin up and a straight back as he led the group, was crumbling before us. Even when he was a child, he had to make mature decisions. He learned to suppress his feelings and to place Ser and our mandate first. It was why I was the first to forgive him when he made the mistake of kissing Ser the summer before high school. It was the first time he'd acted for himself. The first time he showed weakness. I convinced Colin to do the same, and once we did, it was easy for Godric to agree. Now, Kagan looked lost and vulnerable. I had seen this look on him only a handful of times, and it was always because of Serris.

"I think it's time to finally stop this madness before it's too late." Colin gave us both a hard stare as he set his jaw stubbornly.

"Assuming it's not too late," I added.

"How do you propose to do that?" Kagan snapped. "What makes you think she would even listen to us?" He buried his face in his hands.

"We need to meet with the queen's protectors. Perhaps they have advice for us. Or maybe the queen could help us," I suggested.

The three of us looked at each other in silence. I could feel the panic in the air—a sense of urgency to act, coupled with the desire to tear the world apart at the thought of losing our mate.

Even if I have to grovel for years, I will not lose my mate. I knew the guys felt the same; we would stop at nothing. *Serris was ours, and nothing and no one would get in our way in claiming what was ours. Not even her.*

Chapter 5

Serris

"Serris, honey, we need to leave soon. We have a meeting with the other council members. We don't know how long it will last. There's something important the queen wants us to handle. So, don't wait up." Mom looked up from packing her bag.

"Are you gonna be okay?" Dad asked, stopping next to Mom.

"Yep." I looked up from my phone.

"What are you planning on doing tonight?" Mom asked as she put on her coat and handed their office bags to Dad.

"Just hang as usual."

"What about your friends?" Dad walked closer and kissed me on the head.

"They have a party to go to tonight. I'm not allowed to attend those," I said in a sarcastic tone and an exaggerated eye roll.

"Don't start, honey. Lock up." Mom gave me a quick hug, and the two of them left the room.

I didn't move from my spot for thirty minutes. My heart raced, and my palms sweated from anticipation. I sensed the surrounding energy to make sure no one was around my house before I dashed to my room. I had about two hours before the party started. I carefully did my hair and applied my makeup. I put on my top, which I hid under a light workout jacket, pants, and tennis shoes. I then wore a hat and sunglasses to cover my face. Irina had the rest of my clothes in her bedroom.

I've been practicing feeling unexpected energy around me, so I could feel if somebody was following me. When the coast was clear, I ran from our back yard and into the woods. From there, I used Vampire speed to Irina's back yard. She wasn't home, only people she'd hired to get her house ready for the party. I went straight to her room and got changed. I needed to stay put until she gave me the 'go' signal.

My heart was still pounding, and adrenaline still filled my veins when I finished dressing. I paced as restless energy filled me. This was further than we had gotten in the past. Usually, our parents or the douchebags would have put a stop to our plans already. *The fact that I made it this far is freaking great!* Now, the burning anticipation was slowly replacing my restless energy. *I can't believe it! We are actually going to pull this off!* Kier and I will get to spend time together.

My heart thumped, and my stomach twisted as I thought about Kier. *Am I really ready to take the next step with him? I mean, I liked him, but did I really want to be with him in such an intimate way?* "Stop it." I brushed off my second thoughts and the guilty feeling I had. I was tired of being an inexperienced senior who had been sheltered all her life. I deserved to live a little. *I need to do this.*

I clenched my fist and took deep breaths until the nagging worry inside of me was just a nuisance at the pit of my stomach. My parents and the quad had ruined my chance of having a normal, carefree life. This was my chance to experience what every kid in school got to do. *I will not let my nerves turn on me.*

My head snapped up as I heard the music blasting. A broad smile appeared on my face as I slowly felt the energies fill the house. The party had officially started, and I was present. I did a merry dance and then paused mid-dance when I heard a knock on the door. I didn't know if I should hide or not, but then the door opened, and Kier's head popped in between the crack. We both exchanged grins, and he walked inside with a sparkle in his eyes.

"Hi," he said as his straight, white teeth flashed.

"Hi." I smiled up at him. My hands shook and were wet from sweat, which I surreptitiously wiped on the side of my skirt.

"I can't believe you're here." He stepped closer. "You look gorgeous," he said with heat in his eyes.

My eyes dropped in embarrassment, but he cupped my cheek, lifting my face to meet his lips. I sucked in a breath and wrapped my arms around his neck. His tongue invaded mine, and I met his stroke eagerly. We pulled apart, breathless. He placed a few more gentle kisses on my lips, then rested his forehead on mine. Once our breaths were back to normal. We both shared a smile and a chuckle. "We should head down before you tempt me some more," he said as he pulled me out the door.

"Wait. I didn't get the signal from Irina yet."

"They sent me up here. The coast is clear. The quad is far away, busy with some errand from their parents."

"Sweet."

We walked down the stairs, hand in hand, and my face broke into a wide grin. They had transformed the house into a crazy party scene with streamers and balloons everywhere.

Kids clustered in groups with drinks in their hands while some danced to loud music while colorful lights flashed above. Others were on top of the furniture, dancing. The entire room sizzled with excited energy, which energized me. As we descended the stairs, I noticed some couples on the couch and at the corners making out. It added some intensity to the air. The combination of energies from everyone had my veins buzzing. "This is amazing!" It was just as I pictured and more.

I heard a scream as arms wrapped around me. "We fucking did it!" Irina jumped, and I joined her along with Ciaran. "I can't believe you're here!"

"Me too! Thanks to you both!" We had our arms around each other as we continued to jump in triumph.

Irina pulled me into the kitchen, followed by Ciaran, Bret, Kier, and Kristo. She pulled out shot glasses for each and poured witches' brew. My brow rose in surprise.

Ciaran saw my expression. "Bitch, don't tell me you're gonna chicken out. This might be the last time you get to attend a party." He grabbed one glass and handed it to me with a raised brow.

Irina's eyes narrowed. "What he said."

I raised a hand. "Okay. It's just, I don't want to get wasted and make a fool of myself."

Kier wrapped his arms around me and whispered, "I'll take care of you, baby."

I smiled and said, "Okay, let's do this."

Irina raised her glass. "To Ser, and for fooling the loser quads."

"Yes!" I raised my glass.

"Aye," the others said as we all took our shots.

I coughed and grimaced, then looked around in search of water. I gulped half a bottle and coughed some more. "That shit is nasty."

"You say that now, but after the second or third, you won't be able to stop drinking it." Irina smiled from Bret's chest.

"Oh, god. I think I'll stick with human drinks." I looked around the large kitchen island that was filled with an assortment of alcohol. The witches' brew could fuck up any supernatural, unlike the human drinks, which would only relax us in large quantities. Our metabolism was too fast for us to feel the effects of alcohol. However, the witches' brew was spelled. It was costly and scarce.

Kier tugged on my hand. "Let's dance."

I glanced at Irina and Ciaran with a worried frown.

"Don't worry. I overheard my parents talk about the quad being gone all day. Some kind of important meeting. They were worried about someone, and they were assured that someone was not leaving the house."

My jaw dropped, and I made a face of incredulity. "That someone was me, wasn't it? Those fuckers," I hissed.

"Well, we watched them leave for the city, and we haven't seen them return." Irina shrugged.

"You're right. I won't let the quad ruin this party for me. How about we take another shot?"

Everyone eyed me, and then a smile spread on their faces.

"Yes!" Irina pumped a fist in the air.

"Damn, girl," Ciaran smiled.

"Hell, yeah," Bret said.

"Are you sure?" Kier whispered in my ear.

"Shut up, Kier. Don't be a killjoy. Let our girl let loose," Ciaran admonished.

Bret was already passing around shot glasses that Irina filled. "On three." She looked around, raised her glass, and said, "Three."

This time, I didn't cough. However, I could feel the heat on my face. I was also feeling more relaxed.

"Let's dance, bitches!" Irina raised her and Bret's hands and led the way to the middle of the dancing crowd.

Her house had a massive space under the double stairs, which was transformed into a dance floor. Even though the music beat was fast, Kier wrapped his arms around my waist, and we swayed to the music. "Are you okay?" Kier asked over the noise of the music.

I smiled up at him with a stupid grin on my face and nodded.

He returned my smile and leaned in for a kiss. When I surfaced for air, my foggy brain felt woozier from the kiss. This was what I had been missing as I sat home alone. Finally, I was out having fun with friends. This was what I should have been doing all along. Not cooped up at home.

I stayed in Kier's arms and couldn't recall how many songs we danced to. Our bodies took command and danced with the beat—we got lost in the music as our bodies swayed and melded while the rhythm pounded through our ears. I dripped sweat, so it's a good thing I wore a cropped camisole and a short skirt.

Someone tapped my shoulder.

I turned, and Irina handed me another shot as Ciaran gave me a bottle of water. "Drink."

I didn't argue and drank both and turned back to Kier. His cheeks were red, and our eyes locked into one another. "Wanna get out of here?"

I nodded, then Kier led me outside, where there was less noise and fewer people. There were a few kids scattered around the grounds, but the veranda was empty. Each mansion's layout was similar, and we were very familiar with each other's homes.

We stopped at one pillar, then, Kier leaned down and kissed me. My head was no longer swimming, but I had a good buzz going. I felt lighter and was feeling adventurous. Whatever hang-ups I felt earlier were long gone. I wrapped my arms around Kier as he pressed me against the pillar. Our chests rose and fell as our breaths became labored. My head dropped in passion as he kissed his way down my neck. I had never felt this before—I mean, I had shared a few rushed and stolen kisses with Kier, but never this intense. My breath caught, and an unintentional moan escaped my mouth. It was as if my insides were on fire, and every touch caused my skin to sizzle with desire.

"God, Ser. You have no idea how long I've wanted you."

"Shut up and keep kissing me."

He chuckled with his lips pressed against my neck, which caused goosebumps to crawl up my spine. I heard supernaturals were sexual creatures compared to humans, but I didn't know why since I had little experience. *Now I understand.* With our enhanced senses, every touch felt euphoric. Even his smell was intoxicating. My grip on his neck tightened as he ground his hips on mine, causing warmth in my belly. His hand snaked inside my cutoff shirt and cupped my breast as I felt his icy hand on my erect nipple. "Kier," I called.

"Baby. I want you."

"I want you too." I pushed my tongue into his mouth, which started another round of blistering kisses.

I felt his fangs elongate, and instead of being fearful, it heightened the heat inside of me. I tilted my neck to the side as he pressed his mouth on my skin. I moaned as I felt his fang scrape my skin. Vampires no longer use their fangs for sustenance, but we still have them for pleasure. Ancient humans were spot-on when they wrote about the pleasure that came with a Vampire's bite. Modern Vampires now only bite with their partners. A bite means more than the act of sex alone. However, they often go hand in hand.

Perhaps it was the alcohol in me, but the thought of Kier's fangs piercing my skin and tasting my blood had my panties soaking wet. I wanted him to taste me. I didn't care that we were out in the open or hadn't even had sex yet. I needed to feel the pleasure of his bite. He licked and nipped at my neck, and I impatiently pushed his head closer, and my eyes rolled back, and euphoria flowed inside of me as I felt his fang nick my skin.

I heard him moan in pleasure, and his tongue touched my skin. Just when I was about to ask him for more as I felt myself close to release, he was violently yanked off me.

I cried out and saw him on the ground, with Godric choking the life out of him. Kier's face was red, and his eyes bulged out as blood dripped at the side of his mouth.

"Stop! Let go of him!" I pounded on Godric's back, but I might as well be pounding on concrete. He didn't even flinch. I looked around helplessly, but couldn't find anyone to help, so I climbed on his back and pulled on his hair.

I might as well be an annoying fly with how much attention he paid me. He flipped Kier over and whacked his back. Kier spat out a lot of blood and could hardly hold himself up. I jumped off Godric in panic.

"You're hurting him. Let go! Help!" No one was around, and he kept hitting Kier.

Helplessness turned into anger which flooded my veins and caused my eyes to turn. With my Vampire sight triggered and adrenaline flowing in my veins, every detail of blood on the ground and splatter on Kier's face and shirt was precise. My breath escaped as I heard Godric's fist connect to Kier. My breaths came in pants as I clenched my fists. *How dare he! I told them to back the fuck off.* I pushed all the angry energy I had on Godric, and he flew a few feet away, hitting one pillar, which cracked and chipped.

I ran to Kier and helped him sit up. He blinked his swollen eyes, and I wiped the blood that smeared his face. "Are you okay?"

He nodded, then we both glanced at Godric, who was stirring.

My eyes narrowed. I glanced at Kier and helped him stand up. Kagan, Colin, and Liam approached Godric and helped him to his feet. I stepped forward as soon as I was sure that Kier was steady on his legs.

Breaths were coming out of my nose in a hiss, and my fists tightened. "I fucking warned you all," I growled as anger filled me to the brim. I felt the same outrage in my surroundings, not just my own, and I greedily absorbed it and filled my veins as I got ready to battle my foes once and for all. They had crossed the line, and they were going to stop. I could also feel angry energy throughout the entire town and even in Abrea. *I welcomed it and raised my head and basked in the feeling.* The wind whipped my hair as energy crackled around me.

"Ser, please stop," Kagan pleaded.

My mouth twisted, and I spread my arms out and welcomed some more. "You were all warned." My voice sounded unfamiliar—enhanced from the power I had absorbed past the city. *These fuckers were all going down!*

The quad looked beyond me, which made me pause as fear flashed in their expression. I tilted my head and stopped in my tracks. I followed their gaze, and my eyes grew to see all the kids surrounding me, their eyes red and fangs out, ready to tear the quad apart. Adult Vampires covered the grounds' enormous expanse, not just from the party but also from outside.

The shock I felt made me lose my concentration and the hold of the massive energy I had gathered. It left me quickly, which made me see black. The last thing I saw before I passed out was the quad running toward me.

Chapter 6
Colin

I held my head between my hands and pushed off to stand. "Can you all please shield!" Liam had his eyes closed. I was sure he was feeling the same. Whenever the guys were emotional, their shields against Liam and me don't work. I could hear every thought that crossed their minds. I could hardly stand being in my head, let alone three others. Plus, I had been trying to determine if I could hear Ser's thoughts, but it was quiet.

Everyone had the same questions. *Is she okay? When will she wake up?* It's been four hours.

Her parents had been up to check in on her along with ours. The queen summoned us, but Ser hadn't stirred since we brought her to Kagan's house, so we hadn't moved.

Her parents even had the queen's medical team look at her, but we were told she was okay. She just needed to replenish her energy.

That didn't ease our worry. We needed to see Serris awake. I'd rather see her awake and angry than lying limp and unresponsive.

I needed to be away from the guys to mute their constant thoughts, but I couldn't bear to leave her.

Kagan had been pacing at the foot of the bed and would glance up at her each time he passed. Godric sat on the couch on the right and hadn't moved or said a word. His thoughts had been dark. He was still riding the edge of wanting to harm Kier.

I couldn't even think about it. The idea makes me want to join Godric in his plans and murder the fucker. *He dared taste the blood of our mate; there really was no other choice.*

I puffed out a breath and walked to the window.

"Are you sure you got all the blood out?" Kagan asked.

Yes, Godric responded through our link. *I will bleed him dry if I didn't.*

I looked back to study his face, and he met my eyes in defiance. He was serious.

I turned and braced my hands on the ledge. Then, my head snapped toward Ser's direction. It was faint; only our Vampire hearing could pick it up, but her heart rate and breathing changed. *She's waking up.* We rushed to her side as we watched her stir. Then she lifted her hand and rubbed her forehead. She blinked and looked around, then squeezed her eyes shut. She sat abruptly and clutched the sheets as she leaned on the headboard. "What the fuck? Why am I here?" Her eyes narrowed. "Where's Kier? Is he okay?"

I felt a wave of collected anger through the bond as she asked for the guy who dared taste her blood. Liam pushed calming energy through our bond.

"Cut that shit, Liam. I can read your energy, and it doesn't work on me," Ser snapped.

Shock and surprise crossed Liam's face.

Fuck, our influence doesn't work on her, Kagan said.

Worse, she can read our energies, I responded.

"Well?" She raised a brow.

Kagan sighed. "Please hear us out. Let us explain everything."

"Answer my question." She scrambled out of bed and walked to the center of the room.

"We will answer all of your questions if you sit down."

"Don't tell me what to do, Kagan!" Her eyes narrowed.

Kagan's mouth opened and then shut. *Help. I don't know how to talk to her.*

"Ser—" I said.

"Don't call me that. You lost that privilege four years ago. We are not friends. Only my friends can call me that." My chest constricted with her words. It was like a whip to my chest.

Liam's brows knitted as he shared my pain. "Serris. Can we please talk? I know you have a lot of questions, and we have a lot of explaining to do. If you give us a chance to explain, we promise to answer all of your questions. No games."

She faced him fully and cocked a brow. "No games?"

He shook his head.

"No lies?"

I felt hope and relief through our bond. "No. Promise."

"You know, I can read everyone's energy, and I can tell if you're lying."

"We promise," I interjected.

She studied me for a moment, and my heart skipped a beat.

"One lie, and I'm out of here."

"Fair enough," Kagan said.

She threw Kagan a nasty look. *Probably best you say as little as possible. I'm sensing a lot of anger directed towards you and Godric,* Liam said.

She made her way to the couch with arms crossed as she sat and glared at all of us.

We approached tentatively and sat around her.

"Okay, talk." She gestured impatiently.

"First, to answer your question. Kier is fine. He was completely healed by the time we left. Your second question is more complicated." I studied her face and then looked at the guys for help.

She looked relieved to hear about Kier, which pissed me off.

"I suppose I should explain first," Kagan muttered. I could read his thoughts still. It scared him to say the wrong thing and drive her away. "It's complicated," he started.

She tutted in annoyance.

"Wait. I'll explain it." Kagan raised both hands. "I just need to gather my thoughts."

"Start with the break," Godric spoke for the first time since we got here.

Ser's brows rose, and she looked at Kagan in interest.

"The reason we stopped being your friends four years ago is the same reason you're here." Kagan paused.

Ser frowned but said nothing.

"I made a mistake in kissing you four years ago."

Ser snorted and rolled her eyes.

"I mean, I had been dreaming about kissing you for years, and when I did. It was more than I had imagined." The vulnerability was back in Kagan's eyes.

Ser gave him a look of disbelief.

Kagan's lips lifted. "I mean it. I still think about that night. However, it still shouldn't have happened. It was wrong."

She looked up toward the ceiling and let out a deep breath. "You're not making sense. Just spit it out."

"It was wrong because it wasn't the right time. It could affect our future." He gestured to all four of us.

She followed his gesture with her eyes, and her frown got deeper. She cocked her head. "You mean our future?" She gestured to the two of them.

"No. All of us. You, me, Colin, Godric, and Liam. We are all connected, and we needed to stay the course."

"What does that mean?" she said in exasperation. "How are we connected? By hate?" She chuckled.

"Why do you think our parents raised us the way they did? And why us and not the other council kids?" Liam asked.

She shrugged. "Because they are freaking crazy?"

God, I freaking miss her, I said in amusement through our bond. Only she could bring out laughter in me in these kinds of situations. I heard the guys' thoughts lighten up as well. However, Godric was still riding an intense desire to kill Kier.

Liam shook his head, and a smile threatened to break through his lips. "Well, aside from that. They never told you the story of how they became council members, did they?"

She shook her head.

"The queen approached all of our parents on the same night," I interjected.

"Do you know how the queen's powers work?" Liam continued.

"Kinda," she said.

"The queen is named our heart because she is literally connected to all Vampires. She can link to all of us and even share our powers. No matter where the Vampire is located, she can link to them. Even if only a small amount of Vampire blood runs through someone's veins, that person is linked to the queen. At conception, she felt her successor and her protectors." I paused and studied her reaction. She looked interested in the story. I remember how much she would focus intensely and give her full attention to someone telling a story. *I miss that.* My chest ached at the thought.

"Who were they?" she asked with interest. For a minute, it was like she'd forgotten to be angry.

Kagan gestured to all of us.

She frowned. "Our parents are the successor and protector?" Her red lips quirked. I couldn't stop staring at her cupid's bow and her full, red bottom lip. Watching her these past few years and not be able to touch her had been torture. She had developed into an enticing woman. *How can everyone not see the characteristics of the queen?* Long, shiny black hair and bright black eyes, luscious red lips contrasted with porcelain white skin, and a curvy body with a tiny waist. Like the Cantil snake luring its prey with its bright yellow tail right before injecting its venom, she was designed to entice. The queen was filled with allure—her body, face, voice, and movements beguile, but she was the deadliest of us all.

I cleared my throat. "No, our parents were appointed councils, because the queen sensed that they conceived her successor and her protectors."

"You mean...us?"

"Yes," Kagan said.

She studied us closely. I assumed to read our energy. Her eyes narrowed after a minute. "You're not lying. You truly believe what you're saying, or you've gotten good at masking your lies," she said to herself.

Kagan smiled. He looked at her like he wanted to hug her and never let go.

Her eyes narrowed in response, and Kagan wiped the smile off his face quickly.

Liam and I laughed through our bond. *Shut up, fuckers*, Kagan said.

"So, say I believe you. Which I don't, by the way. But let's pretend that I do. What does that have to do with this?" She made a circle, gesturing to all of us.

"Yes. Well, as I said. The kiss was ill-timed because it would have affected all of our futures. You were meant to be with all of us, not just one. If we would have continued down that path, then..."

"What?" She got up abruptly. "What the fuck are you talking about?" She had her hands on her hips and wore a pronounced scowl. "You're all fucking crazy. I'm out of here." She moved toward the door.

We all got up and protested, but Godric's voice boomed. "We can prove it."

She paused and turned with a glare. *Yeah, she's still mad at you for kicking Kier's ass*, I said.

His thoughts conveyed he would have done it again in a heartbeat. He tried hard to suppress his errant thoughts, but he couldn't shake the darkness. Only his need to be close to Serris and his conscience was stopping him.

"How?"

"Take your pick? Did you want to speak to our parents or the queen?" Godric returned her gaze with a challenge.

She was quiet and unmoving for a few minutes. We held our breath as we watched her. Eventually, she sat back down. Liam rubbed on his temples. The constant shift of emotions must take a toll on him. Serris kept us on edge, and I'm sure Liam was being bombarded with all our feelings. "I definitely want proof. I don't trust any of you. But, for now. I have more questions."

Kagan nodded.

"What did you mean exactly when you said, I'm meant to be with all of you? Like, date you one at a time or all at the same time?"

"No. You're not meant to date us," Kagan said, and she visibly relaxed. "You are our mate."

She sat up straight. "The fuck...?" She jumped to her feet, crossed her arms and started pacing. "No. Just no. This is insane. Too fucking much," she muttered to herself. Now and then, she would glance up and would mutter, "Fucking ridiculous."

We didn't dare interrupt. We just watched aptly.

She turned to us and asked, "Why am I here?"

"The transfer of power has begun, and you passed out because you used up a lot of power and it was too much for you to handle since you had very little control. The queen had insisted that we stay close to you now that the process has started. Every supernatural will sense the power shift and will come after you. You're no longer safe," Kagan said.

She held out her hand. "Stop. Just fucking stop. The blows just keep coming. You four just keep fucking up my life, don't you? Now, I'm in danger?" She faced us with clenched fists and stormy eyes, which caused me to hold my breath as I knew that familiar pissed-off look. We had been at the receiving end of Serris' explosive temper, and it wasn't pleasant. She felt so much. She laughed and loved with no abandon, but it was the same with her anger. Perhaps it was another queenly trait.

"Fuck this." She pivoted and marched toward the door.

"Serris, please."

"You're in danger."

We got up to stop her, but she thrust her arms out, and we flew back. She ran out, and we scrambled to our feet to follow. We skidded to a halt as all of our parents surrounded her.

"I don't want to hear it. You are all in this together. Since day one. You are all on their side." She gestured toward us. "My own parents." Anger was coming off her in waves, and her eyes flickered red.

"Everyone just calm down. Let's all sit down and talk. Please." Kagan had both his arms raised like he was facing a dangerous animal.

"Don't fucking tell me what to do!" Serris snapped and flashed out of the room.

"What the fuck?" I looked around in confusion.

"Since when can she flash out?" Liam asked.

"She's the queen. She can do whatever she wants. You boys locate her. We'll contact the queen," Mr. Blackthorn said. The council members filed out in a rush, and we looked to Kagan.

"Okay, we've done this a few times. Just think of her. We should be able to locate her."

"That was when we knew where she was. She could be anywhere. Not to mention, she has gotten good at cloaking," Liam snapped.

"What do we do?" I asked.

"Keep trying," Kagan barked.

I closed my eyes and tried to picture Serris. It wasn't hard to do since she was always in my thoughts. I remembered finding myself in her room the first few months after we cut off our friendship with her. A few times, she brought us to her in her sleep. We would allow ourselves to stay the night when that happened. We would hold her tightly and fall asleep and pretend that our world wasn't falling apart. Eventually, that stopped, but I still couldn't let go, so I would always sneak in and watch her sleep. I wasn't allowed to touch her anymore, but just being near her was enough.

Even if they were unpleasant, the interactions we had throughout high school were a fucking balm to my soul. It was one thing to watch her from afar, but I longed for her to look at me and speak to me. Of course, we had to do our duty, but we were also possessive assholes who couldn't stand any guy looking at, let alone touching, what was ours. No matter how fucked up tonight was, at least she was speaking with us once again. Which healed the million cracks in my soul that had gathered in the last four years.

Now, we must find our mate because it was time to claim her. We had been without her for far too long.

Chapter 7
Serris

I found myself somewhere in Abrea, surrounded by towering buildings and brick roads. I flashed into an alleyway that smelled like excrement and scrunched my nose as I hurried toward the busy streets filled with mostly Vampires, a few other supernaturals, and humans. I was getting a lot of stares. At first, I thought it was because I was still wearing my party outfit, but then I encountered others who wore skimpier clothes.

Then I started reading their energy, and fear flooded me. The Vampires were curious and had a natural inclination to protect me. I drew the other supernaturals to me out of curiosity, but the sinister ones were intoxicated by the power and drawn by greed. Kagan's words echoed in my head. *You are no longer safe.* I wrapped my arms around myself and walked at a brisk pace. I didn't know where I was going or how I even got here. I couldn't flash so I didn't know how to get back.

I refused to acknowledge the creeping thoughts, but they kept nagging at me. *The guys weren't lying.* I felt it in their energy, and this is my proof right here. *Plus, why would all of our parents lie?* Even though I had issues with my parents, they wouldn't go as far as lying about something as big as this. *It makes little sense though. I can't possibly be the queen's successor.*

I just can't, I told myself stubbornly and tampered down those unpleasant thoughts.

The metropolis noise muted, making me realize that I'd left the city center. It looked like I was in the industrial section. I stopped and looked around the empty streets and got an uneasy feeling, so I resumed walking in an unknown direction. I kept glancing back as I felt eyes on me, and I had a feeling someone was following me. As I walked, the feeling got more potent. My eyes darted in several directions as I read their energies. My stomach sank as I realized they were surrounding me.

My heart started pounding, and my adrenaline flushed into my veins. I pulled energy from my surroundings. Perhaps, if the guys weren't lying, it meant I was pulling energies from other Vampires. *Okay, how do I use this power?*

As I walked, I noticed the road ahead was a dead end. I was still several blocks away, but with my enhanced vision, I could tell they would trap me. I stopped and cocked my head, then inhaled deeply and smelled Fae, Shifter, and something else. "Come out," I yelled.

I sensed their energy approach as they surrounded me, and then I turned and instinctively raised my hand and blocked an energy blast from the Fae. I sighed in relief that the energy I controlled did what I needed it to. My rejoicing was short-lived as the three approached. The dark Fae wore a cloak, but the energy I sensed from him was immense. The Shifter was enormous—taller than Kagan and bulkier than Godric. The unknown was scary. He looked like a cross between a mutilated animal and several breeds of supernaturals. His energy was foreign—darker than any sup that I had ever felt in my life—pure evil.

I was truly scared then. My energy would only take me so far. Although my parents had me in combat training, *how could I possibly defeat all three's power? Well, I'll be the youngest queen in history to perish, I suppose.* A chuckle escaped me.

"What's so funny?" Growled the Shifter. His eyes shone yellow, and his claws extended.

"You and your companions. You all look hilarious," I mocked. "Let's get on with it then. What are you waiting for?" I motioned with my hand to come and get me.

"You're brave. I will enjoy sucking your powers dry," the Fae said in a soft voice.

The beast grunted.

I didn't wait for them to make the first move. I blurred behind the beast and punched as much energy into his back as I could. He stumbled and fell forward. The Shifter slashed in my direction, but I was already gone. The Fae aimed another blue energy ball at me that I dodged. I mimicked his motion and lobbed my energy ball, but mine was red. It hit his cloak, and I flashed in front of the Shifter and kicked him with Vampire strength. He grunted and staggered but stayed upright. While I was engaged with the Shifter, the Fae took advantage and shot some kind of magic at me. I hissed in pain as I felt coldness seep inside of me. I gritted my teeth wrapped the Shifter with more energy. As I was about to lob another red energy ball at the Fae, I heard a commotion and massive arms wrapped around me. I struggled for a second, thinking it was the beast; then I glanced up and saw with relief that it was Godric and the guys. He passed me to Kagan, who wrapped his arms around me and flashed us away.

He flashed us into a black marble room with gold and red accents. "Why did we leave? We need to go back and help them." I pushed off Kagan's hold and suddenly felt cold, but I ignored it.

"Your safety is our number one priority," he said firmly.

I flashed him an irritated look and then ignored him. Instead, I looked closely at the room, and with a sinking feeling, I knew he'd brought us to the castle. They were telling the truth. "Where are we?" I whispered. Hoping I was wrong since a part of me didn't want to know and wanted to stay in ignorant bliss for a little while longer.

"The castle," he said.

"Fucking great. Why did you bring me here?"

"Are you hurt? We need to get you checked. We felt your pain."

I rounded on him. "What do you mean you felt my pain?"

"Oh, yeah. We can feel you when you're in distress."

"The hell does that mean?" My hands rested on my hips, ignoring the coldness that seemed to come from my bones.

A tinkling chuckle came from the door. I turned, and my eyes grew. The queen stood by the door with an amused look. There was a man next to her.

"Hello, Serris. It's about time we met."

"Ah..." I didn't know if I should curtsey or bow, so I froze instead.

The melodious laugh came out of her again, and I couldn't help but stare. She had black hair like mine, but hers was wavy. Our eyes were similar, so were our lips and our body structure.

She wore a tight red dress that went down her ankle and flared out the bottom. The dress stressed her cleavage and her tiny waist. We could be related. However, there was something regal and intoxicating about her presence. Even the man next to her was impressive. He was tall, with ebony skin and a firm jaw. He nodded and said, "Princess."

"You can relax." She smiled. "I remember being just like you several hundred years ago. It feels just like yesterday, but at the same time, it seems like an age ago," she said with a sad look on her face, which she masked quickly.

I frowned. "Can you read my mind?" I asked carefully.

She moved toward the couch and sat. She patted the space next to her, indicating for me to join her.

My eyes grew in surprise. The queen of Vampires wants me to sit next to her. *I must be dreaming.*

"No, my dear, but just like you, I am very attuned with the surrounding energy."

I slowly moved and made my way to her. I glanced at Kagan nervously, and he nodded in reassurance. I sat and tried to squeeze myself next to the arm of the loveseat, giving as much space as I could manage between the queen and me.

The queen reached for my hand and came closer. I gasped as our skin touched. Our energy sizzled, and it felt familiar, like she was my long-lost sister. I glanced up at her in astonishment. She grabbed my other hand and her brows knitted together.

"Um, is there something wrong?" I asked carefully.

She didn't respond right away. The man with her left the room, and then her eyes met mine. I studied her in curiosity. But she looked at me with worry. "You were spelled. I can't say exactly what it does, but it's seeping into you slowly." She glanced at Kagan, who gasped. "Tell us what happened," she whispered.

What the...I tried to see if I felt any differently. Aside from freaking out and possibly losing my mind as I sat next to the queen, I felt fine. Well, I felt cold, but that was it. I glanced at the queen who was waiting for me to speak. I studied my hands and said, "I somehow flashed to the city when I was upset and found myself in the industrial section. I felt someone follow me, but I reached a dead end, so I stopped and faced them. Not knowing how I flashed the first time; I had no choice but to stay and fight." Kagan made an irritating sound, but I ignored him. "They surrounded me, and when they finally showed themselves, it was a dark Fae, a Shifter, and a... I don't know what the creature or beast was."

"Beast?" The queen's eyes grew.

"Yes. He had evil energy—something foreign, and he looked grotesque. I took him down first since he seemed the most sinister. We exchanged a few blows, but while I was engaged with the Shifter, the Fae hit me with something. I didn't see it. The entire time he was throwing blue energy balls at me." I shrugged.

"How did it feel? Did it do something to you?" The queen urged as she kept hold of my hand. Her touch felt nice and warm.

"I felt pain initially, and then coldness seeped into me. I ignored it and continued fighting. I didn't feel it again until I was here."

"Jarius went and fetched the healer. The rest of the guys should join us shortly." The queen said.

"Can you tell me what's happening?" I asked.

"I have a link with my mates, but if I concentrate hard enough, I can tap into the thoughts of specific Vampires—something we don't do unless it is essential. Just because we are capable, it doesn't mean we should. Our powers are bestowed upon us for a reason. We don't abuse it, and we always need to think about how it affects those who are weaker than us. The queens are given immense power over the Vampire race. We must not abuse it. We should only use it to protect and never for personal gain."

I frowned and looked down. "So, you really think I'm your successor?" I whispered. My chest contracted in disappointment and betrayal.

"I don't think. I know. You felt our energies, didn't you? They are the same. The transfer of power already started. We will need to train regularly." She reached over, tucking a stray hair behind my ear. "Unfortunately, these are tough times. Someone is determined to take one or both of us down. You must stay here in the castle where you are protected."

I opened my mouth to protest, but the words didn't come out. My entire future flashed before me. I didn't know what to think.

"I know how you feel."

She must have read my energy because I was careful to mask my expression. *How can the queen know how I feel?*

She smiled. "Remember, I told you. I was where you were hundreds of years ago. I had the same feelings. So, there is no one else in the world that understands what you are going through. I will tell you the reason for everything and pass on all that I know in due time. The healer is waiting outside. She will lead you to your quarters, and once you are feeling better, we will resume our training."

I nodded in defeat. *I mean, what else can I say? I can't really argue with the queen.*

"Can I call my parents?"

"I will have them come and visit. Remember, don't leave the castle grounds and don't go anywhere without your mates." She looked me straight in the eyes and waited for an answer.

I took a deep breath and nodded. The queen wrapped her arms around me. "I'm glad to finally meet you. I have been keeping a close eye on you since you were in your mother's womb. I feel like I've known you forever. I hope one day, you will feel the same about me."

Her familiar energy wrapped around me, and I couldn't help but flash her a bright smile. "Thank you."

On her way out, an old lady walked in and bowed.

I frowned and looked at Kagan in panic.

The fucker hid a smile, so I ignored him and turned to the old lady. "Hi."

"Princess. I can lead you to your quarters."

"Oh, you can call me Serris. Please."

"I'm afraid I can't do that. The queen had asked me the same thing when she was young, and I declined as well." She was a short lady with white hair tied in a tight bun. She wore a black button-down shirt and a long black skirt that went down to her ankles. "You've known the queen since she was my age?" *How old is this lady?*

Kagan followed silently, just a step behind us. We walked down more marbled hallways with high stained-glass windows and paintings on the walls. The place creeped me out.

"Yes, I was a young gal, just like you when I started with the current queen's predecessor."

"You mean you've served two queens?"

"I plan on serving three." She grinned.

My face flushed. "I..." I looked away. Still uncertain with the reality that was staring me in the face. It didn't seem real. A part of me still believed there had been a mistake.

I felt her cold, wrinkly hand pat my shoulder. "You will do, child," she said before opening a heavy, carved wooden door.

I wanted to ask what she meant, but my words were forgotten by the gloriousness of the suite. This had an opposite feel from the room we were in a moment ago. This room was white with gold trimming. It was just as opulent, but it was more welcoming than the previous room. There were several couches set around a gigantic fireplace on one side. The middle was a hall that led to several doors, then at the end was some sort of room that had an arch for an entrance. The room looked like a dining room with a large, rich wood dining table.

"Wow."

She led me through the last room with red carpet, and blue furniture, which was sitting across from another fireplace, a desk and chest of drawers. The bed was at the center; it was larger than what the quad and I had.

"I'm sorry. I didn't get your name."

"You can call me, Maybel."

"Miss Maybel, thank you. How long are we staying here?"

"This will be yours until the queen moves out. Then you will decide on a new design for the palace."

My brow rose. "This is my room, and I get to redesign the entire castle? That seems like a waste."

She smiled faintly and gestured for me to lie down. I looked down at my medium-length heels, short skirt, and a cutoff shirt, and she laughed, then motioned for me to follow her. She led me through the doors I didn't notice, and my jaw dropped. The walk-in closet had several rooms—a central one surrounded by mirrors and more seating areas. Then we walked past clothes for guys. "Those are for your mates, and these are yours. Get into comfortable clothes, and I will meet you back in your room.

I had to pick my jaw up off the floor, so I didn't move for a few heartbeats. The clothes were my size, but they were definitely not my style. *Perhaps they were the queen's? But she was taller than me by a few inches, and they were new. Did she pick them for me?*

This is so bizarre. I quickly located some comfortable pants, a sweater, and thick woolen socks. The queen's comforting touch had worn off, and the coldness had slowly seeped back into me. I wasn't shivering, but I was cold. With my warm clothes, I felt comfortable.

Kagan sat on the sofa by the fireplace. The fucker looked like he felt at home. Like he often came to the palace. He was silently chatting with Maybel, which stopped when I entered. I ignored the fucker and lay in bed.

I lay stiff at first, but the bed was comfortable. I sighed and pulled the blankets over me. Maybel sat next to me and smiled. "I'm sorry, child. I can't allow you to sleep." She rolled the blankets down to my waist, and I frowned in protest, but my eyes closed.

"Serris, wake up," Maybel said sharply.

My eyes shot open. "I'm sorry. I'm just so tired and cold," I murmured. My brain felt cloudy. *I just needed to rest for a bit.* My eyes were drifting closed again, and I missed what Maybel said. The bed on the other side dipped, and Kagan grabbed my hand. *Hmm. I didn't want him holding my hand, but he felt warm.*

"Ser. I need you to stay awake. Can you do that for me?"

I shook my head. I couldn't recall why I didn't like it when he called me Ser. I just didn't like it. I felt someone's hand cup my face. It was warm, so I nuzzled next to it as my eyes fluttered closed. Coldwater splashed on my face, and I gasped and sat up.

"What the hell!" I coughed and lifted a shaking hand, pushing the hair out of my face. My sweater was wet, and I was shivering violently. I glared at Maybel, not liking her very much at the moment. "What was that for?" I said in between chattering teeth.

"You were succumbing to the spell. I'm sorry, Princess, but I can't allow you to sleep."

"What do you need, Miss Maybel?" Colin asked, followed by the twins. They looked out of breath like they were running.

"You four, keep your mate awake. No matter what it takes, do not allow her to sleep. The rest come help me gather supplies." She rushed out of the room, followed by three other men.

Liam approached. "Serris, what can we do?"

"C...c...cold."

"I'll get you some dry clothes," someone said.

My eyes were getting heavy again as I leaned on the headboard.

Someone gently slapped my cheek. "You can't sleep, Ser."

"Just a quick nap. I'm so tired."

"Keep her cold."

My eyes fluttered open. "No," I protested.

"Sorry, Ser. We need to take your wet shirt off."

"Isn't that helping? It's keeping her cold."

"It's wet."

"Shh...trying to sleep," I murmured.

"No, Ser. You can't sleep." Someone pulled me to their warm chest, which I gratefully nuzzled.

"We need to take your sweater off."

I nodded, but my eyes were heavy. The cold hit me as soon as the sweater was off. My eyes opened, and I looked up at Colin, who had his arms wrapped around me. Liam was in front, Kegan on one side, and Godric on the other. "Why are you creeps surrounding me?" I asked weakly. I didn't move from Colin's arms, but I was more aware. I shivered, and Liam squeezed to my other side, which pushed Godric lower toward my legs. "Why am I half-naked, and why are you all staring at me, weirdos?"

"How are you feeling?" Kagan asked.

Another round of whole-body chills hit me. The twins wrapped me around their arms like they did when we were younger. I wanted to protest, but their body heat was helping. Only my teeth were chattering now.

"Cold."

"You just need to stay awake until Miss Maybel gets back," Godric said.

"Here, put this shirt on." Kagan held up a white shirt. They dressed me in a thin camisole. "Need more clothes."

"Sorry, Ser. We need to keep you cold. You seem to want to sleep when you're warm," Liam said as he rubbed my arms up and down.

"We need to change her warm pants and take off the socks," Colin said.

I tried to protest, but my eyes were heavy once again.

"Ser, don't sleep."

"Here."

"Ser, we're going to change your pants, okay?"

I shook my head, but they didn't listen.

"Sorry, Ser."

As soon as my socks and pants were off, coldness hit me, which had all of my limbs shivering. "I h-hate you guys." I looked down and saw I was wearing short shorts. "Fu-ucking cold."

"You can hate us when you're alive and well," Kagan, the asshole, said.

"Where are they?" Colin asked.

"They better hurry. We're running out of tricks. She's only coherent for a few minutes."

"I c-can h-hear you, ass-hole."

"I'm gonna go check on them," Godric bit out.

My body was exhausted. So, I leaned on the twins as they rubbed heat into my skin, and Kagan watched with a desperate look in his eyes. We held each other's gazes for a moment, and I saw his raw emotion staring back at me. For a heartbeat, it was like the last four years never happened, but then again, I must be hallucinating. I blinked a few times slowly, and then everything turned black.

Chapter 8
Godric

I didn't need to go far. Miss Maybel and the queen's protectors were walking down the hall. I turned to ask Miss Maybel about Serris' condition when I heard my brother's panicked thoughts. "No." I pushed forward and took off in a blur. Maybel and the queen's protectors were close behind.

I skidded to a halt as cold and heat flooded my system. I didn't feel fear often but seeing your mate limp on the bed and your brothers helpless before her was a sight I would never forget. It took everything in me to reel in the darkness and not suck in every living energy for miles. The dark thoughts of finishing Kier surfaced. *This is all his fault.* My fists clenched, and I exhaled loudly as I tried to control the swirling dark tendrils begging to be set free. *Nothing else matters, only revenge.* There were commotions around me, but I struggled to stay present.

I shook myself from the darkness and turned to Miss Maybel, who used her herbs and trinkets as she mixed her healing energy and used it on Serris while she barked orders for the rest to assist her.

The room muted as I stared at Ser's face. It was only when I looked at her that I felt peace. Without her, my world was chaotic and dark. It was surprising that I hadn't killed anyone when Kagan first had us stop seeing our mate. No one realized then how much I needed her, since it was hard to tame the darkness within me.

Without my mate to balance me out, the darkness would have taken over by now. *I live with no light. It was a constant struggle and war within me.* However, when she was around, I felt like myself again. Without her, I would be the monster I struggled to contain every second. In the past four years, I lurked in the shadows, like a creep—needing to be near her. Just her presence brought peace in me.

If she only knew, she would hate me even more. I needed my mate like I needed the air to breathe. If she didn't survive, I wouldn't be responsible for the monster I'd become. If needed, I would soon follow her since I refused to be separated from my Serris—even in death.

Her body jerked, and I involuntarily took a step forward. A hand clamped down on my shoulder. It was Duncan. He knew what I was feeling and was probably the only person here, aside from the queen, capable of stopping me once I unleashed the monster. "Let them do their job. She'll be fine."

I jerked my head toward his face as he looked me in the eye, conveying the truth. He didn't just say those words to appease me. He truly believed she would survive. A spark of hope ignited inside of me and I let out the breath I was holding and allowed myself to see my surroundings.

Maybel had her wrapped in silver energy that had a faint glow. If I listened hard, I could hear Serris' heartbeat. It was weak, but it was definitely her heartbeat. *Thank fuck.*

The guys tried to give Maybel and two other healers some room to work, but they couldn't stay far away from Serris. I opened my bond to them and heard the worry in their thoughts and emotions. I could pick out their concern easily because they weren't shielded. I was the opposite. *They should never hear my thoughts and feelings when I lose control.*

Maybel and the other two surrounded Serris. They had their hands over her and were chanting under their breath, even my Vampire hearing couldn't hear or understand. Sweat beaded down their foreheads and their bodies were tense from exertion. The light around Serris grew brighter and looked more solid. Finally, Maybel dropped her hand, and so did the other two. She looked exhausted but satisfied. They cleaned up Serris and tucked the blanket up to her chin.

"She needs some rest. It will be up to her to fight the rest of the spell," Maybel said.

"Thank you, Miss Maybel. Can you tell us what they hit her with?" Kagan asked.

"The dark Fae used cultivated magic." She paused and must have noticed the confused reaction we shared. "It means he triggered something inside Serris. Her energy was used against her. He used it to power a simple spell. It was clever really. She was powering the freezing spell he hit her with. Since she is coming into her powers, the freezing spell is deadly. For an ordinary supernatural, it would normally wear off, but for someone with unlimited power..."

"You mean, the bastard turned her power against her?" Colin asked.

"Yes, but Serris is strong. I'm confident she will pull out of this." Maybel reached up and patted Colin's arm on her way out as the two healers followed behind her.

Duncan moved toward the door. "We will give you all some rest, but tomorrow we resume our training."

Our heads snapped in his direction.

Nikolas crossed his arms. "We understand how you all feel, but there is nothing you can do but wait."

"You must be ready. You are no use to the princess if you don't know how to fight her enemies or to help her when she needs it." Gadiel wore a scowl as he walked out, followed by the other protectors. Silence filled the room as we watched our sleeping mate. We trudged toward the bed and sat around her, watching her in silence.

"How long do you think will she be unconscious?" Liam asked.

"It doesn't matter as long as she wakes up." Colin took off his shoes and crawled into bed next to Serris.

Kagan's brow rose as Liam followed and settled on her other side. I hid the smile on my face as I recalled what it was like when we were young, and the twins would sandwich Serris in bed, and Kagan would get annoyed that he didn't make a move first even though he had plenty of opportunities. Throughout the years, we got comfortable with our sleeping spots. The twins on each of her sides, and Kagan and I next to the twins. Sometimes, when someone complained, the twins would stay on the same side, and Kagan and I would interchange in sleeping next to Serris.

The twins gently laid their arms over Serris, but she didn't stir. Something settled inside of me. After four years, everything finally looked right. This was how it should have been all along. Of course, our mate shouldn't be fighting for her life, and she probably would kill us all if we came anywhere near her, but just for tonight, it felt good. I shrugged off my jacket and took off my boots and crawled into bed next to Liam.

Even though each one of us woke up every few hours to check on Serris, it was the best sleep I'd had in four years.

When we woke up, Colin and Liam stayed with Serris as Kagan and I trained with the queen's protectors. We planned on trading in a few hours.

We met at the training room, which was where we'd trained since we were kids. It was a large room with a training ring, weapon wall on one side, sparring mats, weights, and exercise equipment. It had a large space in the middle with wooden floors with different apparatuses for stamina, agility, and room to spar.

Jarius and Duncan were already waiting for us when we walked in. They wore loose-fitting pants and light shirts. We shared powers, which was how the queen's protector was recognized. At birth, the queen would sense the unique abilities and bond the protectors possess. Kagan and Jarius are magic wielders. Other Vampires could manipulate energy or elements, but they could do it all. They could rival the strongest witch or an elder Fae. While Duncan and I have dark energy, we have control over death and shadows.

With no preamble, Jarius said, "We asked you two here to discuss the events that led to the disaster." Jarius had always been serious. Perhaps it was the pressure that came with being the leader since Kagan had the same traits. However, he clearly wasn't pleased with us right now.

Duncan's dark gaze hadn't left us. He crossed his arms over his chest, and his feet spread apart. If I didn't grow up training with him, it would intimidate me. He looked like a wrestler. "Start from the top," he said.

Kagan and I eyed each other and then cleared my throat. "I felt an intense feeling of wrongness and an urgency to get to Serris. Then an intense pain in my neck. I doubled over before I realized what was happening. Her blood called to me. I was closer, so I got to her first." I clenched my jaw as I recalled the scene I flashed to. I could have killed him instantly if it wasn't for the need to get Serris' blood out of him. I took a ragged breath in and continued. "When I found them, I had a strong desire to get every drop of blood out of his mouth. I made him gag until I was certain he spat everything out."

"Are you sure you got every drop out?" Jarius asked with a frown.

I noted the intensity of their expression and raised my brows. "I think so? I didn't really know what I was doing. Everything was instinctual."

Duncan walked to the bench, then sat and asked, "Do you know what it truly means to be the heart of Vampires?"

Jarius followed but didn't sit.

Kagan and I sat on the floor, facing them.

Duncan leaned forward, elbows on his thighs, and said, "We call the queen that because she is literally our beating heart. When our heart dies, so does the power of Vampires. We revert to our mindless ancestors."

"Yes. We know about that." Kagan nodded.

"Okay, but did you know, our core power still lies within our blood. Just because we no longer have to consume blood, we still depend on it. Our queen represents our blood power. That makes her blood very powerful. It is a well-guarded secret that only protectors know about. If another consumes a queen's blood, they become bonded to the queen. If they consume enough, they will become your fifth mate."

"What?" My heart raced as cold crawled up my spine. *What if I didn't get all the blood out?* "What would happen if there was a fifth mate?" I asked.

"Your lives are tied to the queen and her to yours. She needs every one of her mates to guide her and stabilize her power. Without her mates, she risks being overpowered and vice versa. You will perish when your queen dies. A weak mate, one who does not have the added abilities of a protector, will be a liability to everyone and to the Vampire race," Jarius said in an ominous tone.

Kagan searched my face, looking for assurance that I got all the blood out.

I shook my head. "I'm not sure. I didn't know what I was doing. I acted on instincts." I thought hard about what I saw. "He didn't sink his fangs into her neck. I'm certain of it. He just nicked her skin."

Jarius gestured for Kagan to get up. "We will need to trace her blood."

"How?"

"Close your eyes and feel for the bond you feel for your mate."

Duncan gestured for me to stand as well. "You need to practice this as well. You four took too long in locating the princess when she disappeared. It should be instant. Instinctual. Close your eyes and concentrate."

It took me a couple of tries before I could concentrate. I kept trying to rack my brain about the incident.

"Concentrate," Duncan commanded by my ear.

I felt for my bond to Serris. It was easy since I often reached for it when I needed to feel calm or needed strength.

"Okay, now try to pinpoint a location."

"How the hell do I do that?" I almost opened my eyes.

"When you feel the queen, you're actually feeling her blood. Her power is the blood of Vampires. She is one and the same. When she's in danger, you'd be able to flash to her instantly, regardless of the distance. This should be the same with her blood. You were all overthinking it today. It was why it took forever for you to locate your queen. The result was her being attacked. Your delay risked the whole Vampire race. That must never happen again," Jarius said in a firm tone.

Kagan and I wanted to crumble in our shortcomings. Instead, I focused on Serris. I could sense her close by. When I focused on our bond, I just knew where to find her—like our bond guided me. Although, there was a faint nagging feeling tugging at me toward the south. Her blood. "I feel it."

"Good, now go to it, and we'll follow you," Duncan said in front of me.

I hesitated and froze, and then I felt Kagan's reassurance. I thought of going to it, but it didn't work, so I concentrated on the blood, and instead of thinking, I felt myself there. I blinked, and I was in Irina's backyard, standing on the dry blood. Soon, Kagan, Duncan, and Jarius flashed next to me.

"Kagan, I want you to summon the blood to you," Jarius said.

Kagan stepped forward and raised his hand over the blood and closed his eyes. If it wasn't for his stiff shoulders, I wouldn't be able to tell he was performing magic. He was utterly still.

After a few heartbeats, small droplets of blood rose from the dried spots on the ground.

Jarius waved a hand, and an ember flashed in the air, which incinerated the blood. "Now, I want you both to concentrate once again." Jarius crossed his arms.

Kagan and I shared a look. "When the queen's blood has been spilled, you can never be too careful. Always double-check or triple-check if you must. Leave no doubt." Then in a low voice, only we could hear, he added. "Don't give your enemies any hold over us."

I closed my eyes and concentrated. Serris was at the castle close to the twins, but I also felt a very faint tug not far away. Coldness flooded my system, and my eyes flew wide open.

"No," Kagan whispered.

"What is it?" Duncan asked.

"Did he swallow some of her blood?" Jarius crossed his arms as his eyebrows met in the middle.

I shook my head as I studied the ground. I thought hard. "I made sure to get all of her blood from his mouth. It never touched his stomach. I'm certain of it," I insisted.

Jarius waved his hand, and we were back in the training room in the castle. It was disorienting, flashing unexpectedly.

"Kagan, I need you to do a conjuring." Jarius looked serious.

A look of confusion passed over Kagan's face, which Jarius didn't miss.

"Don't call for it. Follow the events with your mind." He paused. He must have seen something I didn't because, he said, "Remember, you have a strong affinity with the queen's blood. Your mandate is to protect the queen. Therefore, there are no restrictions on your abilities to accomplish that goal. You are only limited by your imagination. Trust your brothers when it comes to your mate's blood. Godric says he got all the blood out of the boy's mouth, so find out how he has it so you can plan on extracting it."

Kagan was silent, and then he glanced at me. He had a thoughtful look on his face before he took a deep breath. This time he held his hands loosely to his sides. He didn't move for close to half an hour until finally, his eyes snapped open. He looked at me and frowned. His eyes were stormy, which made me stand and brace myself for the news.

"You're right. You got all the blood out, but he had a cut in his mouth, which allowed a few particles of Serris' blood to mix with his."

Duncan and Jarius stepped closer. "That's a problem," Duncan said with a frown.

"Can't we get it out?" I asked.

"No. Not without killing him," Jarius said distractedly.

My heart skipped a beat. "Will he be a fifth?"

"No. There wasn't enough blood consumed. However, he might have an unhealthy attachment to the princess." Duncan shook his head.

"Will the feeling be mutual?" Kagan bit out.

Duncan and Jarius shared a look. They were probably communicating with each other. "Not really. At most, she will feel a close friendship, but that's it." Jarius tapped his chin. "Keep practicing and familiarize yourself with the connection you have with your queen's blood and send down the twins." He nodded, dismissing us.

We walked back in silence, both in deep thought about the repercussions of Kier's relationship with Serris. Worry filled me as I thought of their already close relationship. *What would this bond make them? I should have fucking killed him. Maybe I still will.*

"This makes our job more complicated." Kagan sighed.

"Do you think there's a chance she would choose him over us?"

He clenched his jaw. "I hope not."

"Yeah." It would not happen. No matter what it takes, we will claim our mate.

Chapter 9
Serris

This feels nice. I felt safe and didn't want to wake up. So I kept my eyes closed, hoping to return to my dream. Although I couldn't recall what it was about, it gave me warm and fuzzy feelings inside. My lips twitched as I nuzzled deeper into the sheets, holding on to the feeling of excitement and giddiness that came with falling in love. *I wish I could bottle that feeling.*

My eyes flew open as I felt a hand slide down my back. "What the hell?!" My eyes grew wide as four bleary-eyed men looked up at me with messy hair. I sat up, abruptly tugging the sheets with me. *The quads are shirtless on my bed.* Heat filled my face as I looked away from their muscled chests with difficulty. "Wha-what the hell is going on?" I said as I scooted up the bed, dragging the sheets farther up to my chin.

"Serris!" Colin beamed and wrapped his arms around my waist. I stiffened up as Liam did the same. "You're awake."

What the hell is going on? Am I still dreaming? Why would I dream about the quad on my bed? They are sexy as hell, though.

I shook my disturbing thoughts away and met Kagan's eyes. "How are you feeling?" he said.

Instead of answering, I glanced at Godric, who had been studying me intensely. My eyes darted down his toned stomach, and I stopped myself before I drooled all over the sheets. *Why are they half-naked and in bed with me?* My face burned as I admired how much their bodies had changed in four years. My eyes trailed Godric's large bulging muscles, built like a wrestler, then moved to Kagan's leaner body. Then I eyed the twins' broad shoulders and thin waist. *God, stop ogling their bodies...I'm definitely dreaming.*

I squirmed as I felt the heat of the twins' arms, which managed to stay wrapped around me.

"What's wrong? Why aren't you saying anything?" Kagan leaned over Colin and cupped my face. I stared back at his golden-brown eyes, but my eyes darted away from discomfort. The look on his face reminded me of the night he kissed me. Liam stirred next to me, which broke Kagan's spell on me.

"Am I dreaming?" I asked more to myself as I studied the unfamiliar room. "Where the hell am I?"

"What do you remember?" Liam looked up, not showing any signs of releasing me.

"If I'm not dreaming, please give me some space."

The twins detangled themselves from my waist, which left me feeling empty.

None of them moved far; the quad surrounded me on the humongous bed.

I remembered the enormous bed in the queen's castle... and my mates. *Fuck!* All the events from yesterday flooded back to me, and filled me with mixed emotions, but the dominant one was a betrayal. "So, everything you said was real?" I whispered.

No one answered. Instead, they stared and regarded me with a careful look.

I studied Liam, Colin, and Godric for any injuries as I recalled the attack. They seemed fine. "What happened to the ones that attacked me?"

"They're gone." I turned to Godric and noted his clenched jaw, which stressed the angles of his face.

"We suspect there will be more." Liam's eyes flashed, which captivated me for a moment. It had been so long since the last time I had stared into his eyes. It was one of the things I loved about the twins when we were young. Their eyes reminded me of glaciers or a clear ocean that changed color from light to dark, depending on their mood. It was enchanting to stare at when they glowed with excitement. My eyes darted down his straight nose, and his moist pink lips twitched as if a shadow of a smile threatened to break free. I trained my eyes at the ceiling as heat flooded me. *Jesus, I must have hit my head or something. What the fuck is wrong with me?*

"Did I really meet the queen yesterday?"

When no one answered, I peeked and caught them exchanging looks. "What?"

"Ser, you've been unconscious for four days," Colin said slowly.

"What?!" My head snapped forward.

"The cold spell almost killed you. We were so worried when you didn't wake up after the first day. Maybel has been checking on you every day. Even the queen stopped by a few times." Kagan said as he laid a hand on my leg, which caused warmth to travel from my belly and into my chest.

I was silent for a moment, trying to absorb their words. "What about my parents?"

"They stopped by often when they weren't busy trying to find your attacker." Colin crossed his arms, which caused his muscles to bulge. Then my eyes traveled down his flat, muscular stomach and down the prominent V shape of his waist. *Oh my god!* My eyes jerked up, and my face flushed with heat, as I realized what I was doing. Colin's mouth turned up as his heated gaze met mine. *What are these guys doing to me? Why am I reacting to them suddenly?* I can't even concentrate on the life-changing events that fucking happened to me. *What is wrong with me?*

"Can you all wear some clothes? Why are you all in bed with me?"

Kagan flashed me his rare carefree smile. "The queen instructed us never to leave your side, and Maybel instructed us to keep you warm." Then he shrugged sheepishly.

"Oh, god. You mean, you all stayed with me. Like this"—I gestured and made a circle—"for four days?"

"You're our mate, Serris," Liam said.

"I'm just going to ignore that statement and take a shower." I got out of bed and looked down at a flimsy camisole and boy shorts I was wearing. I turned to the quad with narrowed eyes.

The twins, who were fairer than Kagan and Godric, had a noticeable flush, while Kagan's ears turned red. Godric refused to meet my eyes. I placed my hands on my hips. "Someone better talk."

"We're sorry. You needed to get out of your wet clothes. We had to do it, but we tried to be respectful. We promise," Liam said.

"You fuckers saw me naked?" My voice rose as I crossed my arms on my chest. I didn't feel violated, which was odd since I hated the quad. I was more embarrassed.

"We didn't look." Colin shook his head.

"How did you change my clothes without..." I turned to hide the look of mortification on my face.

Godric's deep voice cut me off. "Trust me. That was the last thing in our minds. Your life was in danger. Even when you were just asleep, we covered you up with a blanket. We would never take advantage of you, Serris."

I held his eyes for a moment and nodded. The sincerity in his tone had my chest contracting. For four days, the quad took care of me. The thought melted my heart, and desire lit in my stomach. *The spell must have messed with me or something.* I pivoted and tried several doors for the bathroom.

"To your right," Kagan said.

I shut the door with a thud, relieved to be away from their influence. *I needed to think.*

I filled the tub with warm water, bath soap, and lavender oils, then waited for the bubbles to skim the top of the tub. I soaked in the warm water and took my time washing the last four days off me while I sorted out my confusing feelings toward the quad. My fingers lingered around my achy center as I thought of the quad, half-naked with me in my bed. *Jesus, what is wrong with me? I am not attracted to them. I hate them!* I focused on their atrocious actions in the past four years instead, along with their unforgivable lies. Which helped me pull out of this strong attraction I suddenly had toward them. I relaxed into the tub until I felt sane again and wasn't affected by their beauty, which could distract anyone—even me. *I am definitely not attracted to them. Plus, I like Kier. Oh my god. I needed to see how he was doing.* I jumped out of the tub and dressed quickly.

The quad, thank goodness, were dressed when I stepped back into the room. I ignored my disappointment in not being able to see their bodies. I bit the inside of my cheeks and squared my shoulders, annoyed with myself. "How's Kier?"

The twins' eyes narrowed, Kagan's fists clenched, and Godric's energy darkened. My fingers twitched as I instinctively wanted to reach for Godric to comfort him.

"He's fine, back to normal." Kagan briefly met my eyes, and then his gaze dropped to his fingers as he played with his rings. The room slowly filled with anger, but also something else, something more potent. *What was it? Jealousy?*

"What now? Can I go home?"

"No. The queen wants us to train, and it's safer for you in the castle."

I stiffened up. "I can't stay here. We have school."

"Let's discuss this over breakfast." Liam gestured for me to follow him out the door.

I wanted to argue but thought better of it. Liam led us into the dining room, where a breakfast feast was served. My stomach growled at the sight of the food, which gave me a momentary reprieve from my worries. I ate Canadian bacon with eggs, bagel, and a side of fruit. I ignored the quad as I felt their eyes on me and ate my meal.

"Here, you need to drink this." Colin handed me a glass of red drink.

"What is it?"

"Maybel made it. It has your supplement. You've been without it for four days," Colin said between bites of eggs.

I took a sip. It tasted like orange juice mixed with cranberry. I was so thirsty I drank it all up. As soon as I set the glass down, Colin refilled it and then dabbed the corner of my mouth with a napkin. Our eyes met, and I was lost in his for a moment. I looked away and hid behind the glass, gulping down the drink.

"The queen has instructed us to continue our studies in the castle. At least while there's still a threat. We also need to focus on training. The transfer of power makes both queens vulnerable, which puts the Vampire race at risk," Kagan said, unaware of what transpired with Colin and me. He sipped at his cup of coffee, even though it doesn't affect Vampires, and ate his eggs.

I frowned at Kagan. I didn't ask for this. I had plans for my future, and it didn't include the quad. The walls felt like they were closing in on me. My chest tightened as hopelessness filled my stomach. *Stop!* I can't think this way. There isn't much I can do, so I need to suck it up.

I didn't want to place myself at risk, nor did I dare defy the queen's orders. Plus, if I were actually the queen's successor, I didn't want to place the Vampire race at risk. *I have little choice.*

When my heart rate returned at a normal rhythm, I popped a grape in my mouth and tasted its sweet juice while chewing slowly. "Can someone tell my parents to grab my phone at Irina's house?"

The room had visibly relaxed with my statement. I raised a brow in question and took a bite of an apple slice.

Colin flashed me a smile that showed his white teeth, and his dimples flashed on both cheeks. *Why does he have to be so good-looking?* "We didn't expect you to take it so...calmly."

I rolled my eyes. "I'm not an idiot. I don't want to defy the queen and put myself or others at risk." I popped another grape into my mouth. "That doesn't mean I forgive you, idiots." I pushed off to get up.

I had planned to get away from the quad since they were clouding my judgment, but I stopped and looked around when I got to the receiving room. *Where do I go now? Was I even allowed to leave?*

"Serris, wait," Liam called out.

I crossed my arms and narrowed my eyes as I watched them approach. "Are you four just going to follow me around?"

Liam shrugged. "The queen instructed us not to leave your side."

I let a loud breath out. "Surely, you four don't need to guard me all at the same time! That's too much. I'm going to scream if you don't give me room to breathe."

"Serris. Can we please talk about it?" Kagan asked.

"What's there to talk about?"

"We never finished our conversation." Liam sat on the long couch, followed by Colin.

"I'm actually trying to pretend that day never happened, as if I never heard those words. Then I can go back to my life and continue hating you." My expression hardened.

"We're sorry, Serris. For Everything." Colin stood and reached out and stopped himself before touching me. "Everything got out of hand. We were hurting, and..." His hands came up in a pleading gesture. "I'm not saying it justifies our actions, but we didn't know how to do our duties and still keep our distance. We never wanted to do or say those horrible things. We just did it because we were jerks, and we were jealous, and we missed you so much." His last words came out in a whisper. It contorted his face in pain, and his eyes filled with sadness. I had to look away, or I would have draped my arms around him in comfort.

"It's true, Serris. We were hurting just as bad as you. We just handled ours in a bad way. You have no idea how it feels to watch your mate hate you or watch another guy touch her," Liam said, his nose flaring.

"That's the point. I don't feel the same way. Perhaps because this was kept from me my entire life. Even my parents have been lying to me. Everyone I trust, lied to me." I stopped as a horrible thought sank into my stomach. I wrapped my arms around myself tightly and asked with my head bowed, "Did my friends know? Did Kier?" I looked up hesitant, afraid of the answer.

"No. It's a well-kept secret. Otherwise, you would have been a target," Kagan said with a clenched jaw.

They really hate Kier.

I expelled the breath I was holding. *At least not everyone in my life was lying to me.* "Who else knows?"

"The school staff. They had to be made aware to help keep you safe. The queen bound them to their word," Kagan said. I glanced at Godric, but as usual, he only looked at me and said nothing. He was riding subtle, dark energy, as he wore a blank expression.

"Why did the queen want to keep this a secret?" I asked casually, but inside I wanted to scream.

"She will need to give you an explanation. All we know is that our parents were told it was imperative that you were not made aware. We grew up being reminded of that fact."

Kagan met my eyes, unapologetic. If there was something I admired about him, he took his position seriously. I always had to remind him to enjoy himself a little when we were younger and not be so serious, but he would always tell me it was his job as a leader. Now I understood what he had meant. Guilt nagged at me because, unlike them, I had a normal childhood. However, I couldn't get past the betrayal—the lies. I might forgive them for their asshole attitude in the past four years but lying to me my entire life was painful.

"I don't know what to think," I murmured. "What are we supposed to be doing now? Can we even leave the room?"

"We should hear from one of them soon. In the meantime, we can discuss a schedule. If you want us to back off, we can do two at a time." Kagan looked around.

Everyone nodded. "We're going first," the twins said at the same time.

"No, you two need to train. Kagan is meeting with Jarius briefly. I'll take the first shift." Godric flashed a full smile. I sucked in a breath. It was rare to see him smile, let alone a full one. *He is breathtaking. He really looked like an avenging angel.* He had a chiseled jaw, high cheekbones, straight nose, and thick shapely brows—he didn't look soft; he looked dangerous. People avoided him and didn't look him in the eyes, probably because he wore a permanent scowl on his face and was large and muscular. However, I'd always seen right through him; he struggled with his powers, so he had to be in control all the time. There were only a handful of times I'd seen him genuinely relax. Sometimes his powers would overwhelm him, and he needed just to be held. I think my talent with energies helps calm down his darkness.

I averted my eyes, but not before catching the mirth in his gaze. *Fucker knew the power of his smile.*

"Okay, we will leave you two. Then we'll trade off after training," Liam said.

"Why can't we train later? We just trained last night. I want to go first." Colin didn't get up.

Kagan rolled his eyes. "Can we not make this difficult?"

"Fine," Colin snapped and followed his brother.

"I will send Miss Maybel over and see you two in a few hours," Kagan said as he walked out the door. He paused as his hand laid on the knob. "Serris," he said, looking back. "I'm sorry for all the horrible things I've done and said these past four years. Please know I didn't mean any of them."

My eyes grew in surprise. He didn't wait for a response and stepped out the door. I looked at Godric to see that he had the same reaction as me. *Kagan never apologizes.* When we were kids, he would always say that a leader never apologizes. Then he'd jut his chin out stubbornly. *He makes tough decisions and needs to stick with them. Apologizing is a weakness.*

"I'm in a fucking alternative universe, where everything is unfamiliar." I sighed as I sat down.

Godric chuckled.

See what I mean? I wanted to say it out loud, but I wasn't ready to go back to our old relationship. Instead, I eyed him warily.

His lips split into a smile. "Why are you staring at me like that, Princess?"

"Princess?" My face scrunched. "No. Just no."

He laughed.

"And stop doing that. It's unnerving. Since when did you start laughing and smiling?" A smile threatened to burst from my lips.

"Do you like it?" He leaned forward as his dark eyes held mine.

My stomach fluttered. I shook my head. "No. I don't." I broke our eye contact, but my heart still hammered inside my chest. I heard him chuckle, which made my stomach contract. *Fuck me. How can I survive being around them?*

I stood up and walked to the bedroom to get away. After a few steps, I paused and turned, then bumped into Godric. He grabbed my arms to steady me as I held in an inaudible gasp, then my eyes met his molten eyes. All I could think about was his closeness and the warmth of his touch. He moved to lean closer, and my body responded automatically and moved closer. Right before our lips touched, my brain caught up with me, and I pulled away. *What am I thinking?* "Don't follow me." I breathed.

He opened his mouth to argue, but I raised my hand to stop him. "No."

I rushed through the door and slammed it in his face. I closed my eyes and heaved in a deep breath. *I need to stay away from them, or my resolve will crumble.*

Chapter 10
Serris

Maybel had cleared me to train; however, my excitement was short-lived. When the queen first saw me, she gave me a smile of relief and held me in her arms. Then she said, "I'm glad you're feeling better, Serris. I knew you would pull through. Before we train, you need to learn about the history of the Vampire queens." She smiled and squeezed my hand before getting up. "Remember, you need to stay in the castle and stick with your mates at all times." I bit the inside of my cheeks and nodded.

She left, followed by Jarius while Nik stayed behind.

Nik led me and the quad to the library, then pointed to the large, thick tomes I needed to read. *She wants me to read all of those?* My eyes grew, and I groaned internally.

Nik didn't smile, but his eyes brightened as if he was holding in a laugh at my expense. *Great! I'll be stuck in this damn library for days!*

I sat heavily on the chair, and he stacked the enormous books in front of me. "Have fun, Princess," he said and strolled out. I curled my lip as I watched him leave and then saw Godric hide a smile. I rolled my eyes and turned to the stack in front of me, then grabbed the book on top and opened the heavy cover.

It was titled *Queen Rosalind* in gold letters. Underneath it, in wavy, handwritten black ink, were the words *my life*. I squinted to see if someone scribbled on the ancient tome, so I flipped the pages and noticed the same handwriting. After reading a few pages, I looked up in amazement and met Kagan's and Godric's eyes. I ignored them and looked back down at the book.

I didn't want to share my amazement with them, but Queen Rosalind had handwritten her thoughts throughout the whole book. I grabbed the other books and realized they were all the same. Each queen had their thoughts written in the books. It was like their own personal account of events and behind the scenes not accounted for and not documented, were all in here. *I can't believe I am privy to this kind of information!*

I devoured the first few pages; some parts of the book were interesting, but some were a drag to get through.

I ignored the quad as best as possible as they each switched off every few hours sitting in the library with me. I felt their eyes constantly on me, but I paid them no attention.

"Serris?"

I looked up from reading Queen Rosalind's fight with the Shifters, which was common Vampire knowledge, so I wasn't surprised to see that she wasn't fond of Shifters.

"Your parents are here. Would you join them for lunch?" Liam asked.

Thank fuck. I need to get out of this room. I nodded and stretched my arms as I got up.

They were waiting for me on the balcony. The twins bid their goodbyes, but I knew they lurked nearby.

"Hi, sweetheart." My dad gave me a tight hug.

"Are you okay?" My mom tucked a hair behind my ear.

I nodded and bit my lip as my excitement in seeing them was waning. I wanted to scream at them and ask why they'd lied to me, but I held myself back. I didn't want to fight since I hadn't seen them for days.

"How are you holding up, kiddo?" Dad passed me a plate of salad.

I took it, scooped some onto my plate, then took a small bite of my sandwich, chewed slowly, and shrugged. "I dunno. My life has been turned upside down. Some crazy beast attacked me, and I almost died. My enemies are somehow my mates. And everyone knew about this except for me. Aside from that, you know, everything is peachy."

I studied their reaction. They glanced at each other, and then my mom plastered on her fake smile. "I'm glad you're fine, sweetheart."

I clutched at the napkin on my lap and glared at them.

"We'll have your schoolwork sent to you. We had your phone, computer, and some of your stuff sent up to your room." Dad cleared his throat and scratched his brow.

"That's it? You're both going to sit there and pretend that everything is fine?" I threw my napkin on the table. Suddenly, my appetite was gone. "How could you sit there and be fine with lying to me my entire life? Your own daughter! You were open with the quad, so why not me?" My voice rose at the end.

"Honey, please. You know we couldn't. The queen instructed us."

"I see." I stared at both of them, giving them one more chance to provide me with a better explanation, but they said nothing.

"Thank you for bringing my things. I need to get back. The queen assigned me a lot of reading." I pushed the seat loudly and left without looking back. All four of the guys joined me after a few feet. I sensed them wanting to say something, but I ignored them.

I stacked the books in front of me so I wouldn't see the quad. Then I spent the rest of the afternoon reading about the seven queens. I cheated and used Vampire speed to get through each tome in decent time.

My lousy mood continued as I read about the depressing accounts of each queen's life—a problematic and dangerous reign and a rough transition to the position, which was the common theme.

I grudgingly could see why the queen thought it was vital for me to read each tome. Each queen imparted essential knowledge from their reign. It also explained her reasoning why she wanted to keep my future a secret from me. My annoyance with my parents and the quad thawed a little as I read about Queen Vida.

I peeked at the quad surreptitiously, and a pang of guilt hit me, but I couldn't bring myself to say anything. Queen Vida was the fifth queen who grew up as a princess; she was spoiled and lacked compassion toward regular Vampires. They dubbed her as the tyrant queen. Even though the queen's nature had always been to protect her subjects, she made unpopular decisions. She justified her cruel choices for the greater good.

Since then, it was decided to make sure the next ruling queen should experience a normal life.

"How are you doing, Serris?" I looked up and found Queen Illeana in front of the enormous desk. She walked behind me and read over my shoulder. "Did you start with Rosalind?"

I nodded. "I was curious. Are these the queens' journals bound to the history books?"

"Yes. The castle's historian starts the binding when the transfer of power starts. Henry has been hard at work since the first power surge."

"Power surge?"

She sat on one chair, then waved a hand that shifted the books to the side and smiled. "Yes, it was sometime this year. You expelled an extensive amount of power, and whenever that happens, it weakens me."

My eyes grew.

"It has been happening on and off over the past month." She chuckled. "Now I know what Anthea meant."

"I'm sorry." I frowned.

She shook her head and flashed me a warm smile. "It isn't your fault. It's part of the transition. It honestly is not bad. More of a nuisance. It's darn inconvenient when it happens in the middle of a fight, I tell you."

"How can I stop it?" I twisted my fingers and looked at her hopeful.

She shook her head in sadness. "I asked the same thing once. This isn't a life I would wish on anyone. I'm sure you know what I mean after reading each queen's thoughts."

"Yes." I studied my hands and peeked at her from under my lashes. "I now understand why you wanted to keep the truth from me."

She reached over and placed her hand over mine. Every time we touched, it felt comforting. Like something connected us. "I'm sorry. You must feel betrayed by the people you care about the most, but it was necessary."

"Queen Vida's decisions were unpopular, but I can see how she thought she was doing the best for the greater good."

"Do you think she was right?"

I thought for a minute. "No. I don't think mass execution and stripping Vampires of their land were the best solutions. It was an easier solution, and I can see how she wanted to make an example of them. Still, she didn't stop there, and the worst part is, she abused her power and used it against her people."

"Exactly. Our powers are not ours. We are simply their keeper. We must only use our power to protect our people and not abuse it. It is a privilege that we can share their powers."

I nodded. "Does that mean I will get to read your journal soon?" I smiled.

She smiled back and said, "I will present this to you during your coronation. A queen's journal is special. It contains information only the queens are privy to. Even our mates aren't able to read the books. The historians and the castle's head spell weaver place unbreakable enchantments on them using the queen's blood. A protector supervises it." She stood up and gazed down at me. "When you're done reading, come find me, and we will proceed with the next training."

"Can I ask you one other question?"

She paused, but I hesitated and eyed Kagan, who wasn't far from us. She followed my gaze and waved a hand. "You can speak freely. He won't be able to hear us now."

"About the...Ah...the mates?"

"What do you want to know about your mates?"

"Does the bond take away my free will and override true thoughts and emotions?"

"Oh, goodness no. Even though you have a natural attachment to your mates, the deep feelings of love and physical attraction develop independently. Keep reading about Queen Una's history. She had a rocky relationship with her mates. That's why she took on a lover." She flashed me a sympathetic smile. "I was lucky to grow up with mine and didn't have the unfortunate difficulty you five have. My relationship with each of my mates progressed naturally to what it is now."

"What if our relationship doesn't progress?"

She studied me for a minute. "It would be unfortunate if you never experience the joy of being mated. It's one of the genuine miracles supernaturals get to experience." She paused and gave me a sad look. "There has never been a queen who hasn't been mated with her protectors. However, I don't see it as being mandatory. As long as you have a good working relationship with them, they should be able to do their job. I don't see why it won't work. It might make their jobs harder, but I can see it working." She flashed me a sad smile, moved to turn, but then stopped. "For your sake. I hope you develop a bond with your mates. It's one of the few good perks of the job. Without them, I wouldn't know how I could have survived all these years." She turned and walked out of the library, followed by Gadiel.

I looked in the direction she'd disappeared to; my gaze frozen on the spot long after she was gone. The conversation made me uneasy.

I stayed for another hour, rereading the section about the previous queen's entry about mates, and then slammed the third book closed in frustration. Queen Illeana was right about the importance of the mate bond. There was also mention of the bond getting more potent along with the transfer of power. That explained my inexplicable reaction to them.

I took Queen Opal's tome with me and followed Kagan back to our room in silence.

Although my body felt exhausted, my brain was reeling with all the information I had learned today. "My queen," Kagan said, which snapped me out of my thoughts and made my head jerk in his direction.

My stomach did a flip-flop inside of me. It bothered me to be addressed as such, but at the same time, the possessiveness in his tone made my veins burn with desire. "Please don't call me that," I whispered.

"You are my queen." His eyes bore into my soul, which lit my insides on fire.

He cleared his throat and asked, "Didn't you want to eat?"

It took me a moment to respond. "No. I'm tired. I think I'm just going straight to bed. Thank you for asking." I turned and ignored the others.

I walked into the room and shut the door. I let out a deep breath as I looked around the empty space; I was alone for the first time, which felt peaceful. I walked around and looked back toward the door. A pang of loneliness hit me. *It's stupid. This is great since they are always hanging around, staring.*

I busied myself reading about the third queen who had a turbulent relationship with her mates. Their enemies took advantage of their discord and were able to get to the queen—her protectors weren't able to save her. In the end, her mates shared their life force to prolong her life, just enough to give the infant successor a chance to transfer power. They died before her, instead of all of them passing at the same time. I was in tears as I read her last entry about how much regret she had with how her relationship turned out with her mates and how much she loved them, and how she wished she'd had another chance. Her last sentence stuck out the most—*I long to be with my mates in the next life and start anew.* Their sacrifice had been worth it as the baby they saved—Queen Una—was famous and known as a mighty queen, and her people loved her.

I rubbed at my tired eyes, so I laid the book on the side table and got under the sheets.

I must have drifted off to sleep because I woke up to a rustling noise. I froze, but then it stopped. I relaxed and closed my eyes. *There it is again.* It was toward the bottom right of the bed. I lifted my head slightly to see, but everything was still. Now it was on the bottom left side of the bed.

"Will you two idiots, stop squirming. You woke her up," Kagan snapped from the couch by the fireplace.

I could see in the dark with my Vampire sight, but Kagan still turned the light on. I blinked and saw Godric lying on the other couch next to him. He had his long limbs folded in an uncomfortable position, and so did Kagan.

The twins groaned from the ground, and eventually, their heads peeked up over the bed. "Sorry if we woke you, Serris," Liam said.

I sat up and leaned on the headboard. "Why are you two down there?"

"There's no other room on the couch. I'd rather sleep here than sitting up," Colin said.

"I meant, why are you here. Aren't there three other rooms in this wing?"

Colin shrugged. "We all wanted to sleep here. We didn't think you wanted us sharing your bed, so…"

"Are you guys for real?" I lay heavily on my pillow, and eventually, I heard everyone do the same.

After a few moments, Kagan turned off the light. It took less than fifteen minutes before the twins tossed and turned from the ground. I placed a pillow on my head to drown out the noise, but it was no use. I couldn't sleep. I felt guilty sleeping on a giant bed as they lay on the hard ground.

I slammed my hands on the pillows. "Okay, you two can sleep next to me," I groaned. "Let's start with just two. Kagan and Godric can go take the other rooms."

The twins jumped onto the bed as soon as the words left my mouth. In the dark, I could tell Kagan wanted to complain, so I said, "You two will be useless tomorrow if you're tired."

Godric got up and left the room, then after a moment's hesitation, Kagan followed shortly.

I turned to the twins, who both watched me. "You two stay on your end," I commanded.

"Good night, Serris," Colin said.

My lips turned up.

"Goodnight, Serris," Liam said.

I closed my eyes and tried to sleep, but now I was very aware of two gorgeous boys in bed. "Are you two dressed?"

"Do you want us not to be?" Liam asked.

I responded by hitting him with a pillow.

"Why are you thinking about our state of clothing?" Colin asked.

"I just wanted to make sure you two weren't half-naked in bed with me."

"Aren't you supposed to be sleeping, Princess?" Colin had his head propped with his hand as he watched me intently.

Perhaps this was a bad idea.

"Go to sleep, Serris. We won't try anything, and we are appropriately dressed," Liam said.

I closed my eyes, but I could feel their eyes on me. "I can't sleep if you two won't quit staring."

"Sorry." Colin flipped the other way, and Liam did the same thing.

After a few minutes, my body cooled off, and I could finally occupy my mind with other thoughts. I didn't think about the twins' broad shoulders, firm chest, and tapered waist. *Jesus, it's useless.* My face heated as I thought of the two of them doing things to me at the same time. *Where is this coming from?* It took me a long time to stop thinking about the three of us. I had to focus on what I read to distract myself from the twins until I finally drifted to sleep.

I woke with the same warm and safe feeling as yesterday. I smiled and felt something tickle my neck. I opened my eyes and felt Colin's breath blowing into my neck; his arm was draped over my stomach, and my leg was on his thigh.

Liam's face was by my breast, and my arm stretched over his head. His arm was wrapped on my hips.

I closed my eyes and groaned. I clenched my thighs as my nipples pebbled.

I caught Colin's sharp intake of breath. His head lifted, and he looked down at me with heat in his eyes. His hand crept up my stomach and touched bare skin. I sucked in a shaky breath but didn't stop him.

What the hell am I doing? I'm angry at them. Plus, Liam is on the other side.

My brain screamed for me to stop, but my body buzzed with overwhelming desire. He slowly traced my skin, lifting my camisole. My chest's rise and fall got more pronounced, and my nipples peeked through the thin camisole. He watched my stomach and then my chest and finally my mouth. He kept eye contact with me as he leaned down slowly as if giving me time to change my mind. However, I was long gone from thinking. I was just feeling, and what I felt was freaking intense.

His touch left my skin sizzling. He leaned closer, and I opened my mouth and met his tongue. A sigh escaped him as we both leaned into the kiss. His hand brushed my nipple as he moved to cup my cheek. Heat filled my stomach, and I moved to drape my arms on his neck, but I remembered Liam. I pulled away from Colin and met Liam's molten gaze.

He was frozen as his grip on my hip tightened.

Instead of feeling embarrassed, I noted my panties pooled with desire. My breathing came in short and shallow. His fingers dug into my waist, and he used his other hand to pull me to his mouth roughly.

Colin started kissing my neck. *Jesus, both the twins, are kissing me at the same time.* It was just as I imagined last night, only better. I groaned. I didn't care if I was loud. Their touch and their mouths on me ruined me forever.

I thought the moment with Kier was intense, but it didn't even compare to this. Every touch on my flesh sent a shot of desire through my system, and my nerves sizzled with heat.

Colin grabbed my face and pulled me to his lips. The twins kissed me with enough passion to light up an entire country. They kissed like they couldn't get enough of me. It was gentle and bruising at the same time. They nipped and licked my skin, which left trails of fire that left me combusting with desire.

Liam traced his nose on my shoulder, pulling down the camisole strap and slowly kissing the top of my chest. He continued to lower the camisole, and I felt the cold hit my nipple, but his warm wet tongue quickly replaced it. I gasped in Colin's mouth and arched my back. I wanted to beg for more but grabbed Colin's nape instead.

I squirmed as tension built in my limbs. Colin yanked the camisole and ripped it off. He palmed my other breast, and I lost it. I leaned back and exhaled a moan.

Colin pinned me down and swallowed my loud moans with his mouth as they both abused my breasts with either their mouths or their hands; I lost track.

I felt a pool of wetness between my legs as I continued to writhe underneath the twins.

"Fuck, Serris. We can feel you and smell your desire," Colin whispered as he kissed down my neck.

"Fucking gorgeous," Liam whispered. I was topless and exposed to the twins, and instead of feeling embarrassed, I liked how they were looking at me.

Colin reached for my breast with shaking hands and soon followed with his mouth. My eyes fluttered, and my back arched. I clenched my thighs as the feeling got intense.

I bit my tongue to stop the scream as I grabbed both their heads and begged. "Oh, god. Please." I didn't know what I was begging for, but I couldn't stand it, and I didn't want them to stop.

"How far did you want to take this, Princess?" Liam asked.

"We don't want you to regret anything. You're in total control," Colin said.

"I...I don't know." I can't think. "Don't stop." *Wait, did I want to have sex with both of them? I don't know. I just need them to ease the ache.* "I'm not ready to have sex...." I took a deep breath to clear the cloud of desire fogging my brain. I bit my lip as I lifted my head and rested my weight on my elbows.

Colin smirked. "Lay down and get comfortable. Do you trust us?"

I thought for a minute and nodded my head.

"Have you..." Liam started.

"Oh, god." I covered my face.

Someone traced a finger on my stomach and in between my breast, which made my breathing quicken. I dropped my head on the pillow and watched Colin.

"Don't be embarrassed, Serris. You're our mate. We're here to please you. We haven't been with anyone else."

I cocked a brow. "You four, haven't?"

"Nope." Liam made the P pop at the end.

"But..."

"You're our mate. We have no desire to be with anyone else."

I frowned. *Why did I desire to be with Kier? Or did I?* I mean, our kiss and his touch didn't feel like this.

"Stop overthinking. I don't want to ruin the moment," Liam said.

"Relax, Ser. We'll ease your pain," Colin commanded.

I hesitated. The twins shared a look, and Liam kissed me, and Colin popped a nipple into his mouth. In no time, I was back to squirming and ready to combust. The twins felt the same, but different at the same time. It was like they were meant to work together.

"Did you want to come?" Colin whispered as he nipped at my neck.

I nodded and clenched my thighs. I felt like one-touch was all it took for me to combust.

"Have you ever?" Liam asked again.

I shook my head.

Their faces broke into identical smiles. *God, the twins, were gorgeous.* I reached for Liam's face and kissed him. He pulled me up, so I was sitting in front of him. Now I could reach and tug off his shirt. I traced his muscles, which had him moaning, and felt Colin lift me as he sat me on his lap. He was shirtless behind me. His naked chest, flushed against my back, felt intimate. I also felt his rock-hard bulge on my ass through the flimsy boy shorts I was wearing. I ground my ass on his cock. We were all moaning and panting as hands and mouths were on each other's bodies. Colin brushed my center with his finger, and I sucked in a ragged air.

"Did that feel good?" He whispered, and I nodded. Colin leaned us back slightly as Liam spread my legs apart. Liam pulled the shorts to the side and rubbed my center. "Dripping wet," he said.

Colin reached over and pulled my shorts off. I was completely naked in front of the twins, and I felt sexy. Colin and Liam worked in a rhythm that had me screaming out a release in just a few moments.

I lay in bed, entirely spent. The twins gave me only a few minutes to recover, and they were on me again. We explored each other's bodies like we had been deprived of something vital for so long. It wasn't until Kagan banged on the bedroom door that we got up.

Chapter 11
Serris

My face flushed every time I saw the twins. Good thing I had been busy, and they mostly left me alone to finish reading the tomes.

I was at a section about boring politics. I read through that quickly and slowed at an entry about Queen Una that made me feel slightly guilty. She was the fourth queen who had a lover drink her blood before the mate bond solidified. This resulted in a fifth mate, which had been proven to be a liability to her and her protectors. It was unfortunate what happened to him. He had to be secured and not allowed ever to leave the castle. He had to be protected, but he was practically a prisoner for several hundred years. Her successors had since then learned more about the bonding via the queen's blood. Apparently, the bond could be stopped if done early after consumption, or the only choice was to kill the person before the bond forms. *Thank goodness Godric stopped Kier and me when he did.*

When it was Godric's turn to follow me, I didn't know how to broach the subject. Guilt ate away at me. I hadn't forgiven the quad and my parents fully, but at least now, I understood their actions. I felt guilty for the lengths everyone had taken for me, including my parents. I just had a lingering hurt, I needed to process.

We were walking down the hall, and I surreptitiously glanced at Godric as I twisted my fingers. He suddenly grabbed my arms and turned me to face him. "What is it, Princess?"

I looked up, and words got caught in my mouth. His face was only a few inches from mine. If I leaned forward, our lips would touch. He glanced down on my lips, and my hands went up to rest on his firm biceps. "You've been glancing at me for a while now. You clearly want to say something."

I didn't realize we were walking back toward the wall until my back hit the cold cement. I flinched and leaned forward. The next thing I knew, Godric's lips were on mine. I froze for a moment, but soon I was gasping for air as he slowly parted my lips with his. He leisurely took his time in exploring my mouth, which felt just as intense as the animalistic desire the twins elicited. He held my face between his giant hands and angled my head so his tongue could go deeper.

My greedy hands explored his large, bulging muscles. My fingers grazed his firm abs, and I heard him suck in a breath. He pulled away and leaned his forehead to mine. We stayed still for a minute as we calmed our racing hearts.

He held my hand as we walked back to our wing. I smiled at our clasped hands. *How did I go from being mad at them to this in less than twenty-four hours?*

He peeked at me, and his lips twitched. My heart fluttered at the sight; it was rare for Godric to relax, and it always brought contentment in me whenever I saw him calm.

It should disturb me to be quickly slipping back to my old place with the quad, but it was like I didn't have control when I was around them. The pull was too strong, and it was impossible to fight. My mind and my desires were in a constant battle.

"I wanted to say that I understand why you did what you did with Kier. I...apologize that you had to see that. If I would have known..."

He placed a kiss on my hand that he still clasped. "Thank you for saying that." After a few minutes of silence and a noticeable tension from Godric, he said, "Of course, you will have to forgive me if I end up killing him when I see him."

I squeezed his hand. "No need for that. I promise it won't happen again."

His body relaxed a little, but I could still feel the darkness within him. "You've been keeping your tension bottled up again," I stated without looking at him.

I felt his eyes on me, and then finally, he said, "Can you feel...the darkness?"

I peeked at him and nodded.

He sighed and opened the door to our wing. "It's difficult sometimes. However, I have better control than when we were younger. Duncan has been teaching me exercises to recognize my trigger so I won't get overwhelmed."

"I'm sorry these past few days have been stressful."

"It's not your fault. This is what I was born for. If I can't handle this, then I won't be an effective protector."

"You're too hard on yourself. You all are." I walked to the window and looked out at the rose garden. "I know that you have all faced this situation your entire life and that you have had to make adult decisions from the beginning. Meanwhile, I'm mad because you all hid a secret from me—which actually enabled me to have a normal childhood." I leaned on the glass window and tried to make out the people on the grounds. "I feel guilty that I'm upset, but I can't help but feel that way...you know?" I glanced back at him, and he gazed at me.

"I think what you're feeling is normal. The conflict inside you means you are compassionate, but still true to yourself. It's scary when someone who will be as powerful as you felt in absolutes. If you feel conflicted, then you probably will make the right choice."

I turned to face him fully. "That's the thing. I don't feel like the successor. I'm just me. I'm still waiting to wake up from this nightmare, to be honest."

He flashed me a smile that made my stomach flutter. "That's what's going to make you a great queen, one day."

"You think so?" I peeked at him from under my lashes.

"I know so." He tucked a hair behind my ear and trapped my eyes with his. His hand lingered on my neck, and then he traced his fingers slowly to my shoulder. Tingles traveled to my belly, and goosebumps peppered my spine as he continued to trace a finger on my chest at a maddening pace. Then he proceeded down on my breast and circled my nipple on top of my shirt. I clenched my thighs and leaned into the wall to support my weight. My eyes fluttered, but I kept them open. He held me captive, and I couldn't look away. I tightened my hold on his arms as his hand kept traveling down my stomach then between my legs. He kept up with the same speed over my clit. My leggings' thin fabric allowed me to feel his talented fingers, which had me breaking eye contact as I moaned.

His fingers stopped moving, and he ran his nose on the side of my neck and whispered, "I need you to keep your eyes on me, Serris." My head fell back to the wall as his hands snaked inside my shirt and massaged my breast. His hips ground on my center, which elicited more warmth in me.

I need one of the quad to fuck me soon. They are driving me crazy.

I wrapped my legs around him as he captured my lips, and this time we weren't gentle. Godric tore my shirt off along with my bra. He kissed my breasts, slowly, savoring them.

He set me down and took my leggings off, then stepped back, and his eyes slowly raked down my body and then held my gaze captive with his once again. He stepped between my thighs and spread my legs.

His expert fingers made me forget we were in the living room. "Fuck, Godric." My fingers dug into his arms, and for a moment, my eyes fluttered, and I noticed Kagan over Godric's shoulder, sitting on the couch rubbing himself. Our eyes met, and my orgasm escaped in waves. My limbs convulsed as Godric held me in place. When I could finally stand on my legs, Godric placed a firm kiss on my lips. "You're beautiful, Serris."

My cheeks warmed and my eyes darted to the couch, but Kagan was gone. I wanted to ask Godric if he knew, but I stopped myself. I was ashamed of how much I liked him watching us as he touched himself. *Why did he leave? Did I imagine him being in the room? Why didn't he join us? Oh my god, did I really want him to join us? Fuck! I have four mates.*

Instead of fear, I felt excitement and impatience to be with my men. *I wanted to experience being with them fully.*

So much for being mad.

I had finally finished reading the tomes last night.

After breakfast this morning, I got word that we were starting training. So, I had been eagerly awaiting Queen Illeana in the receiving room. Even the twins' touch couldn't distract me from my excitement, nor did Godric's heated stares.

I hadn't seen Kagan since the incident. I almost asked the others about it, but I didn't know how to bring up the subject. I was sure the twins would understand since we had been getting comfortable with each other behind closed doors even though they had been taking it frustratingly slow.

The knock on the door pulled me from my anxiety over Kagan. I turned as Gadiel walked in and then led us to the queen's private receiving room.

"Serris, come in and have a seat with me." Queen Illeana patted the space next to her.

"You three come with me. She will be safe with Jarius and the queen," Gadiel said.

The twins and Godric kissed me on the cheek before nodding to the queen and Jarius, then left with Gadiel.

"Now that you've read the tomes, you have a better understanding of a queen's life. You also know there is no preparation for politics. However, I could still impart some advice. Trust your instincts and your mates, consult with your advisers and always rule with both your brain and heart."

I stared at her, wide-eyed. *Is she serious? I knew nothing about politics. She can't expect me to know what to do.*

She chuckled softly. "Forgive me. It's been years. I've forgotten what it was like to be in your shoes. What I meant was, there is no preparation for how to deal with other rulers or how to treat your subjects. There is no one way to resolve conflicts or tackle a problem. Now, with running a castle, we have capable people in place who are very good at what they do. They will guide you in every step." She placed her hand on mine, then fixed an intense gaze on me. "A queen's crucial role is to protect her people. Oh, you also have to attend the pesky Rulers' Consortium meetings routinely," she said with her nose scrunched in distaste.

I shifted my weight on the couch. Every word coming out of the queen's mouth had me wanting to run as far away as possible.

"Serris, I need you to close your eyes and take a deep breath." She took both my hands and held on.

I eyed her for a moment and then did as she commanded.

"Good. Now, feel for the energy inside you. Do you feel it?"

I opened my eyes.

"Keep your eyes closed."

I shut my eyes and felt for the swirling energy inside of me, begging to be released. It was like my energy represented the panic I felt from the queen's words—it felt combustible.

"Nod if you feel the energy."

I nodded.

"Good. Now, do you feel how little control you have over it? It's leaking off of you. I can see how much effort you are using to keep it leashed, but if you lose your concentration, it could be disastrous."

I clenched my fists, the skin-tight over my knuckles, which I'm sure she felt. *What is she talking about?*

"Try to let the energy out."

How do I do that? I feel like the energy is flowing into me without my control. How do I reverse it? I shook my head. "I don't know how."

I felt the queen squeeze my hands. "Serris, open your eyes."

I blinked and saw the frown on Queen Illeana's face. "Do you know what our core power is?"

I shook my head.

"A Vampire's core power is fueled from the blood. Our ancestors were predators who craved blood. Although we've evolved and no longer drink blood for survival, our powers have changed little. The core power a Vampire possesses is always predatory. For example, magic wielders pull energies from their surroundings, while your mate Godric takes life energies, the twins take emotions or thoughts. As the queen, you have an innate knowledge of how to use these powers. You are intuitively pulling your subjects' powers and skills into you."

I frowned. *That doesn't sound good.*

"What's important is for you to learn control. The rest will come naturally. Don't pull too much. Just learn to control it."

"How do I do that?"

"Don't fear it and stop doubting yourself. The energy is eager to do your bidding. Command it."

That is easier said than done. I eyed her skeptically, then closed my eyes. *Okay, I felt the energy from my surroundings flow into me. She said I should stop it. How the fuck can I do that?*

I squeezed my eyes tightly shut and locked my muscles. *Stop*, I commanded.

I felt the energy sizzle on my fingertips, then it slowly eased. Good, that worked. *What's next? I have too much inside of me, so I need to release some of it.* I pursed my lips and let out a breath, thinking of release—the same way a balloon deflates. Slowly the energy lessened. I sighed as the pressure inside of me dissipated, and my muscles relaxed.

"That's it. You did great."

She had me practice manipulating the energy until I could control the flow easily. Until it felt natural—a part of me, something that required little thought. Which, admittedly felt better than the suffocating effects I had to endure.

After a few hours of practice, my powers felt natural. From there, it was easy to pull the borrowed powers, as she said, when I borrowed a gift, I handled every power as skillfully as the owner who had trained all his life. I flicked my fingers and lit a small fire. I spread my fingers out, and the fire grew into a small ball. I made it dance around my hand and tossed it in the air, making it grow bigger.

"That's fantastic. You're doing great! Remember, your blood connects you to each Vampire. Their powers are inside of you. Embrace it, and don't second guess yourself. With this knowledge, trust that you are capable of anything you desire."

I extinguished the fire on my hand and replaced it with a snowball. I flashed the queen a big smile, which she returned with a chuckle.

Chapter 12
Serris

Finally! With everything that had happened, it took me a few days to remember to charge my phone.

Lead filled my stomach as I scrolled through the missed messages and missed calls. My phone dinged from texts and missed calls from Kier and a few from Ciaran and Irina. The last message from Ciaran and Irina made me promise to call as soon as I was able—that was yesterday.

Kier hadn't stopped calling. *My goodness. Was he okay?* He'd been blowing up my phone every hour, sometimes several times an hour. I typed up a message to send to Ciar and Ili when the phone rang.

"Hello."

"Oh my god. Ser?"

"Kier? Hi."

"Finally. Are you okay? I thought you were mad at me. What happened?"

"Whoa, slow down. Yes. I'm okay. Are you?"

"Yes. I'm fine. It's just...last time..." He trailed off and a heavy pause filled the line.

"Yeah, I know."

"What happened?"

"I...It's been crazy, Kier. It's hard to explain. I can't even wrap my brain around it."

"Okay," he said in a careful tone. There was an uncomfortable silence between us.

"Is it okay if we don't talk about it? I promise to explain everything when I'm ready." I got up and walked toward the window, away from the quad. I knew they were hanging on to my every word. I kept my back turned to give the semblance of privacy.

Kier didn't respond right away. "Are you sure you're okay?"

"I'm fine. How are you? Last I saw you...you were almost unconscious." I turned and glared at Godric and met his eyes in challenge instead of remorse. My face flushed.

I turned back and faced the windows. "...healed after a few hours, but then you were gone. I thought something happened to you. I've been worried sick."

"I'm sorry. I couldn't call right away."

"Are we okay, Serris?"

Fuck! I don't know how to answer that. I bit my lip and glanced at the twins. They both had their arms crossed and wore an identical scowl. It was like everyone was waiting for my answer.

"Hello, Serris. Are you still there?"

"Kier, I have to go. Can I call you in a bit? I promise we will talk more."

"Oh. Okay, I...guess—"

"Thanks. Bye." I disconnected before he said anything else. I leaned my head on the cold glass of the window. I knew it was cowardly of me not to give him an answer, but I didn't know the answer myself.

After being intimate with the twins and Godric, I should have told Kier there was no us. I didn't know what held me back. Perhaps it was the finality and acceptance of this new life. I didn't know. I dreaded facing the quad, but with a sigh, I turned and found them staring at me.

Kagan stepped forward. "Why didn't you tell him to take a hike?"

I crossed my arms in response. "And why should I do that?" He was right, but I hated his bossiness, and it made me want to challenge him. I haven't seen him in over twenty-four hours...since he watched Godric and me, and these were his first words to me?

He narrowed his eyes as we held each other's gaze. I briefly saw hurt and hesitation before he covered it up and walked away.

I let out a loud breath and waited for the other three to say something.

"You can't keep him, Serris. You know that, right?" Godric said in a quiet voice, then followed Kagan out.

I waited for the twins to say something, but their expressions were unreadable as they stayed silent, which was worse than if they'd yelled.

I sat down heavily on the couch. Guilt and anxiety weighed heavy in my stomach. After a few moments, Colin sat next to me, followed by Liam, which eased the knot in my gut.

"Did you want to keep him?" Colin took my hand and interlaced our fingers.

I thought about it. Kier and I danced around the idea for four years. It was fun and exciting. The build up and anticipation was definitely a significant factor. *Would we have had something?* Perhaps if the quad weren't in the picture, or maybe if they didn't occupy my heart first. Because whether or not I'd like to admit it, they'd always been there. Yeah, they broke it, but they never left. Even in the last four years, they made sure they made themselves known. I was hurt, and it was because I felt so deeply for them that I was hurt. If I didn't love them, then I wouldn't have cared. They broke me when they left. They'd left an enormous gaping hole in me, and I wasn't the same again.

Now, I felt whole. Denying them meant denying myself from healing. It was like saying I didn't want my pieces back together because they were a part of me, whether I liked it or not. They'd always been part of me, for as long as I could remember.

The question was not whether I wanted Kier over my mates. It was whether I was brave enough to put myself out there and possibly have my heart torn out of my chest again because I wouldn't survive it if the quad broke my heart again.

"No. I mean, it was so new. We were still trying to figure out what we were to each other before all this happened. I understand why I can't have him."

"Then why didn't you tell him?" Liam asked.

"It wasn't about him." I looked down and rubbed Colin's hand on mine. "Everyone was waiting for my answer. The answer seemed less about Kier and more about me, you know?" I looked up, searching his eyes, hoping to see understanding. In just a short time, we've picked up where we left off. This should frighten me, but it felt right. For the first time in a long time, I felt safe and complete—like something had been missing inside of me, and now I felt whole.

Colin squeezed my hand for reassurance while Liam said, "We understand. However, it's not fair for Kier. You know he can't get involved. You've read about Queen Una, right?"

"Yeah."

"It's not safe for you, for us, or the Vampire race."

"I know." I thought of Queen Una's lover and his horrible fate. I wouldn't subject someone to the same fate. Then I remembered the last time I saw Kier and how weird he was acting over the phone. My hand flew to my mouth. "Oh my god. Did Kier? Did he—"

"He didn't ingest your blood, but some of it mixed with his through the cut in his mouth." Liam's jaw clenched.

"What...What does that mean?" My hand gripped his arm as fear flowed in my veins.

His hand lay on top of mine. "It's fine. There wasn't enough to have a significant impact."

Thank goodness. My heart settled.

"However, he might...develop a certain attachment to you." Colin frowned. I glanced at Liam and didn't miss the scowl he quickly tried to hide. *Boy, this might be a problem.*

"Can we do something about it?"

Colin shook his head. "No. It's too late."

"How will this affect him? Will he be able to have a normal relationship, or will this affect his judgment?"

"For his sake, we hope so," Liam said darkly. "As for his judgment, we don't think it will be a problem."

"What are you going to do?" Colin asked.

"You're right. It's not fair to Kier." I leaned on the sofa heavily. "I need to talk to him. If you're asking about something else, I need time."

"Fair enough."

My brow furrowed at the thought of the bond possibly swaying my decisions.

Liam peered at me with a look of concern. "What's wrong?"

"Nothing."

Colin poked my side, which made me crack a smile and flinch at the same time. "Tell us what's wrong, or I'll tickle you."

I scooted closer to Liam and raised my hands to ward him off. "Nothing."

He leaned closer.

"Okay. Okay. I was just wondering if our bond was swaying my decisions. One minute I hated you a lot, and the next, I'm in bed with you." I shrugged, and then my gaze shifted from his. "Then I remembered what Queen Illeana said and the story of Queen Una. But everything's happening so fast, and it's hard to believe any of this is real."

Colin lifted my chin and didn't let go until my eyes met his. My breath caught when I saw his emotions written on his face. I wanted to grab his face and kiss him deeply but held back. For a moment, I felt scared. I didn't want to believe it was real. *What if the quad left me again?* A crippling fear filled me.

Liam shifted and moved in front of me, taking my other hand. "Serris, baby. I never get a read on your emotions. You have a natural talent for keeping us out, but sometimes when you're feeling strongly about something, we would get a glimpse of your thoughts or emotions. Just now, I felt your fear, and it felt like a stab in the chest. I can't tell you how sorry I am...we are, for what we've done. We were young and stupid and chose the easy path. It's something we will regret for the rest of our existence. We knew deep inside that what we were doing was wrong. We knew we should have stayed with you. Although, we never really left. You just never knew we were there. So, please believe me when I say that we will never leave you. Even death cannot separate you from us. We are your mates, and we will be by your side. Always." He kissed the back of my hand, and I sucked in a stuttered breath.

"I really should be angry that you four stalked me, but I feel like a part of me knew you were there. I could have sworn I felt you guys around."

We all shared a chuckle.

The queen and I had been training daily. She'd been happy with my progress and had me testing out the different Vampire powers so I would know what was available to me. It gave me a glimpse of the quad's powers, which made them more admirable.

This morning, the queen had an emergency meeting with the other rulers, so she canceled the training. We were under strict orders not to leave the castle. Plus, Jarius told the quad to keep me happy and not trigger any potent emotions because it left the queen vulnerable. I asked to come with her since I learned from our last session that we could share powers when we were together—it amplified our abilities. Everyone assumed the queen was at her weakest during the transfer of powers, but both queens can join powers.

Queen Illeana insisted we stay safe in the castle. She emphasized that the meeting would be brief and that we would resume our training tonight.

I reached out to Irina and Ciaran since I didn't want to sit around all day in awkward tension with the quad. The twins were fine, but Godric had been acting weird since I spoke with Kier. Kagan was still avoiding me.

I got up and left the receiving room and went to the bedroom to wait. I couldn't stand another look from Godric or Kagan. I couldn't tell if they wanted to kiss me or wanted to throttle me, or maybe it was both. Either way, their mixed energy was enough to have me marching out of the room.

I lay heavily on the bed and closed my eyes. I tested the energy I had, and I was pleased I had reasonable control, even if I was annoyed. I felt the bed dip and a rough hand brush the hair off my forehead. My eyes fluttered open, and I saw Godric leaning over me. He traced my jaw with his thumb and then my mouth. "I'm sorry I've been acting weird. I'm trying to cope with your relationship with Kier."

My brows drew together as I saw the pain in his eyes. "I'm sorry I didn't break it off with Kier, but it wasn't because I wanted him. I just needed some time to adjust to the whole mate thing. Everything is going so fast. I just felt on the spot. I promise I don't want to be with him."

He leaned into my hand and kissed my palm. His shoulders visibly relaxed, and he trailed kisses down my arm, starting with my wrist. He then captured my mouth. I leaned into his kiss and sat up and took his shirt off as I straddled his waist. I eyed his defined chest, mesmerized by his muscles. My hand lifted, and I trailed his six-pack with my fingers. I heard his breath hitch. I pressed my mouth onto his neck and slowly licked his salty skin. He pulled on my hair, tilting my head back, then kissed me hard. I pulled away to take my top off when a loud knock had us freezing in place. Before either of us moved, the door opened, and Kagan walked in. His eyes narrowed, and his jaw clenched.

"Your friends are here," he said in a sharp tone. He didn't look at me as he spoke. Instead, he spun and left the room. I glanced at Godric and noted the frown on his face.

Before I met with Irina and Ciaran, I straightened up my clothes and fixed my hair, but I couldn't do anything about the flush on my face. My steps hesitated as I saw Kier with them. I looked around, and sure enough, the twins wore an identical scowl. I looked back, and Godric froze behind me with his fists clenched. Kagan leaned by the door with his arms crossed and his leg propped. *Okay, this is awkward.*

"Oh my god. Ser." Irina threw her arms around me.

Followed by Ciaran. "We were so worried about you."

"I missed you guys." I hugged them back and I blinked hard as unshed tears burned my eyes. Something inside of me settled. The last few days had been difficult. It felt like a recurring nightmare, and they were my anchor to reality. I opened my eyes and saw Kier hover behind them. I smiled.

"Hey, can I have a hug too?" he said with a flash of his charming smile. It constricted my chest in sadness. I draped my arms around him and buried my face briefly as I blinked away more tears that threatened to fall. *We never had a chance, him and I.* We had been trying for four years, and when we finally had a chance...this happened. He didn't deserve it. He was a great guy, and now he will be tied to me forever because of my blood.

I heard a door slam, which made me jump away from Kier. I looked back and saw it was Godric retreating to the bedroom.

Kagan had his feet spread apart and his entire body tense. He looked like he might attack Kier. My eyes grew, and I looked to the twins for help. They didn't look too happy, but they met my eyes and nodded. Colin walked to Kagan and whispered something. He nodded, and they walked inside the bedroom. Liam stayed behind.

"What the hell is going on?" Irina whispered, louder than she intended.

"Let's sit, guys." I gestured to the couch. "Liam, can you please give us a moment?"

His eyes hardened, but I gave him a pleading look. He flashed me a look that said he'd be close by, and I didn't have long. I flickered a grateful smile.

Ciaran laid a heavy hand on my arm and cocked a brow. "What's up with you and the quad and this?" He gestured to the room.

"I don't know, guys. I don't even know if I believe all of it yet myself, but I owe you guys an explanation. Especially you, Kier." I laid a hand on his arm, and he covered it with his hand. I smiled sadly and pulled away slowly.

His smile faltered. *Okay, I can do this. I owe it to him and to the quad. They've stuck with me through all these years.* "Weird things happened at the party. I don't know how much you remember." I looked up at Kier from under my lashes, then gazed at Irina and Ciaran.

They shook their heads.

"Well, remember the weird powers I've been having?"

This time they nodded.

"Well, I now know what's going on. As I said, I'm still wrapping my head around it, but I'm the queen's successor, and the quad are my protector mates." I held my breath, scared of their reaction.

They all shared a frown, then Ciaran's face grew into shock, Irina's jaw fell, and Kier pushed off and said, "What? What do you mean, mates?"

"I'm sorry, Kier."

"Wait, you and the quad? Like all four of them?" Ciaran asked.

"You're the next queen? You're the next queen! Holy shit! My best friend is the next queen of Vampires!" Irina said with a broad smile.

"You get four mates! Bitch, how the fuck?!" Ciaran shook his head.

I shook my head and chuckled. My chest felt lighter. I didn't know why I thought they wouldn't understand. I glanced at Kier.

"Kier, can we talk about this?"

He walked to the window. I followed him, but he kept his back turned. I reached out and hesitated. But I studied his hunched shoulders, and his bowed head and my chest contracted. I laid a hand on his back. "Kier. I'm so, so sorry. I didn't know about any of this or the quad. Otherwise, I wouldn't have started anything with you. I promise I wasn't leading you on or anything. I really liked you."

He leaned his head on the window with a thud. I rubbed his back, and he turned to look at me. "That sounded so final. I guess that answers my question. There's no hope for us, huh?"

"I'm sorry. It's messy. I don't want you tangled in this. It wouldn't be fair to you or them."

"What if I don't care?"

"You say that now." I chuckled darkly. "Trust me, Kier. You're a great guy. You will make a girl very happy one day."

The pain emanating from him was too much. I pulled him in for a hug and held on. I pulled his pain away, and I felt his arms tighten around me briefly. "Thank you, Serris."

"You're welcome, Kier. Remember, I'll always be here if you need me."

He nodded and pressed his fingers to his eyes. He sniffed and kept his head bowed.

I left and gave him some privacy. Liam caught my eyes, and instead of triumph as I was expecting, I saw understanding. My heart softened toward him. It helped me not displace the shitty situation and blame the quad.

Irina pulled my hand to sit next to her. "So, tell us everything."

"We mean everything. Don't leave out any details." Ciaran winked.

My face flushed, and I rolled my eyes. I told them everything, except the intimate details with the quad, out of respect to Kier. Plus, I knew the quad was listening to every word.

I had to pull some of Kier's sadness a couple of times, but eventually, he joined in on our conversation. I felt lighter for the first time since I got here in the castle. I really missed them. I was so happy to be reunited with them.

"You should have been there, Ser. Ciar had a full-on meltdown. We had to chase him."

"Shut up. I did not."

"Did he not, Kier?" Irina turned.

"Yes. The whole school saw."

"Shut up you two. It was so worth it, and the make-up sex was amazing." He fanned his face with his hand.

I laughed, then straightened up. I felt a sharp pain in my chest and cried out and then heard voices around me, but it was as if they were far away. I couldn't see them. I could only see a beam of bright light permeating darkness. I blinked, and the searing pain got worse, and energy flowed into me in droves. I had no control of it, no matter what I did.

I gasped but couldn't breathe. It felt like I couldn't take in much air. I took shallow breaths in but still couldn't feel like I had enough air. I felt like I was dying. I could no longer hear the voices, and I could only see the light getting brighter. I didn't know where I was. The pain intensified. I wanted to scream, but I didn't have a voice. I tried to move my muscles, but I didn't have a body. I was floating, and there was only pain—it felt like I was being burned alive. I arched my back, and my limbs started twitching. I cried out, and everything turned black.

Chapter 13
Serris

*S*erris.

Ser, wake up.

Love, can you hear me?

Babe, come back to us.

I can hear you.

Serris! The quad chorused.

What happened?

Open your eyes, love. Why did Colin's voice sound so sad?

You can do it, baby. Come on. Even Liam sounded lost.

Serris, come back. Asshole Kagan always sounds angry. What was it about now?

Ser. Open your eyes. My eyes fluttered open, searching for Godric. I felt his darkness—it filled him, and he needed me. I tried again, but it felt like my muscles weren't working like my body wasn't responding to my commands. I tried raising my arms, but nothing.

I can't. What's going on?

Serris, listen to me. Follow my voice, Kagan said. I felt his worry, and what else is that? It drew me in. The feeling felt potent and enticing like it promised safety and home. I didn't know what I was doing; I just followed it, or maybe my consciousness merged with it. I didn't know since I wasn't aware of what state I was in, but eventually, I saw the same bright light. However, it wasn't as bright as it was previously. I reached out to it and felt Kagan. I felt his worry and intense feeling of love and protectiveness over me.

Then the light got brighter, and I felt the twins and Godric. I felt their love for me, and the light shone brighter, drowning out the darkness. I blinked and opened my eyes. I first saw Kagan's face, his red eyes, and a five o'clock shadow. The twins looked pale, and their hair stood in different directions. Godric had a dark glint in his eyes like he had allowed the darkness to take over. I reached over and cupped his cheeks. "What did you do?" I whispered.

He leaned into my hand, and a tear fell on his cheek. I sucked in a breath as I felt his turmoil. I kissed the tear away and pulled the darkness off him. He bowed his head on my chest, and his shoulders shook. I rubbed his back, and the twins leaned their heads next to mine. Their arms snaked around me, clutching me tightly.

"What happened?" I asked Kagan, and I reached out with my free hand. I wasn't afraid to reach out to him. I felt everything he hid inside. I also saw behind the brave mask he always wore.

He reached out a shaky hand and clasped mine. I had to enforce my fingers with power. With how strongly he was clutching my hand, he would have broken some bones. However, I didn't complain. It felt like he needed comfort. I shook Kagan's hand and raised my brows. "What did I miss?"

"We thought we lost you," he whispered.

Not again. "What happened? What about my friends?"

"Everyone's fine. They're outside, waiting for you to wake up," Colin said.

"Don't do that to us again, Serris. I can't handle it." Godric raised his head and wiped his eyes.

"What did I do? What happened?" I clutched his hand.

"The queen is dead," Kagan said.

I pulled my hands away, but they wouldn't let go. I felt a coldness flood inside of me. "That can't be," I whispered.

Liam kept an arm wrapped around my waist and the other played with my hair as he avoided my eyes. "They were attacked on their way back from the council meeting along with a few of the other royals who also lost good people. Queen Illeana died three days ago in an ambush, along with her protectors. They didn't stand a chance. She refused to leave and insisted on closing the portal. She sacrificed her life to save many."

Tears streamed down my face. "I should have been there. We were stronger together. I'm not ready. I..." *Oh my god. I can't be the queen. She couldn't be dead, and she was going to retire with her mates. She had plans...she was so close.* I got up, detangling from the quad. My sadness and fear quickly turned into consuming anger. "Who was responsible for her death?"

The quad simply stared as I narrowed my eyes and cocked a brow. If they didn't tell me, I would find out on my own, and I would make them pay.

"Ser, are you okay?"

"No, I'm not okay," I snapped at Godric.

They had shocked looks on their faces.

"What?"

Colin pointed at me. "You're glowing, and your hair is moving like there's wind, but there's no air in here."

"It's creepy, Ser. Stop it," Liam said.

I frowned; anger dissipating from me. I looked down and noticed I was still wearing the same clothes from when I blacked out. I didn't see what they were seeing. I looked up in confusion.

"You just made it stop." Kagan stood up and eyed me up and down. "You look different. You still look like you, but your hair is darker, and your skin is fairer. Your lips are redder, and your voice changed slightly. You look more like the queen. How do you feel?"

"Well, a second ago, I was fucking pissed. I will hunt down whoever is responsible for the queen's death." Anger flowed into me once again. I pivoted and marched toward the bathroom and turned before I shut the door. "When I'm dressed, I want to speak with whoever has intel on who was responsible for this act of war towards our people. I want to meet with them in the throne room." I said it with a voice of authority.

I stayed under the shower, unmoving. I quickly went from sadness for the queen's death, to worry about my new role, then to anger.

What the fuck is going on? Am I going crazy? Why are my emotions out of whack?

I didn't want to acknowledge it to Kagan, but I felt different. Aside from my emotions flipping quickly, power thrummed in my veins, begging to be released. I could sense the thoughts and knowledge of every Vampire in my subconscious.

I still felt a sliver of me somewhere, mourning the loss of my planned future and the carefree life I had. I wasted my time being angry with everyone for not telling me who I was, instead of enjoying the last moments I had of being normal. It was all thanks to Queen Illeana. She gave me the best gift—a chance at a normal life. *Now, I will never get the opportunity to thank her.*

Tears flowed and mixed with water as I cried for the queen, her mates, and my old life. I saw now how much I needed my mates. I needed them to keep me grounded and to remind me of who I was, so I wouldn't lose myself completely.

I picked from one of the dresses that were still in a bag. It wasn't like Queen Illeana's, but it was more my style. It was a long black dress with the sides cut that showed my hips and had a slit that showed my upper thigh. I wore pointy red boots and braided my long black hair to the side.

I ignored the shocked stares the quad threw at me. Instead, I used our link, something I could now access easily. *Come, mates. We're going to hunt down some murderers, and we're going to make them pay,* I said on my way out of the room.

I ignored their feelings of worry about how I was acting and thrill at my use of the word mate. I didn't have time for our relationship at the moment, and I needed to deal with this, so I ignored their weird looks.

I stepped into the receiving room, which had gone silent. My steps faltered as everyone went down on their knees—my mom and dad, Irina, Ciaran, Kier, their parents, and the quad's parents. Then they murmured, "Queen Serris."

I froze for a moment and looked at the quad for help, but they only gazed back at me with pride. Embarrassment seeped into me. "Please stand. There's no need for that." I briefly forgot about my anger and need for revenge.

They stood, and Mom and Dad came over and hugged me. Then everyone in the room took turns, telling me how happy they were to see that I was okay. I smiled and hugged everyone back, then said, "Thank you. Everyone's concern touches me, and I wish I could stay and chat, but I must deal with this." I turned to the quad. "Are they ready to meet with me?"

"Actually, the council is all here. They would know."

I looked around the tight space. We needed a more comfortable room to discuss important matters. I closed my eyes and thought of the castle, and there it was. The layout came to my mind. It was freaky how I could access information instantly. If I wanted to, I could trace where the information came from, but the deeper I dug, the more I would access the person's thoughts and memories. And the queen warned me not to invade anyone's privacy, so I wouldn't do it unless necessary. I waved my hand and flashed us to the room where the queen regularly held her meetings as I heard a collective gasp.

"I apologize. I should have warned you all. I figured this was a better room to discuss such matters." I sat in the queen's chair, and my mates sat on each side of me. The council members—our parents—looked startled but made their way to their seats while my friends stood awkwardly, looking lost. "You guys may stay."

"We usually don't allow outsiders in on our meetings," Mr. Morelles said, the oldest council in the group.

"I appreciate the input." *Please call whoever else needs to be present at this meeting in this room*, I asked Kagan through the mate link. He got up and left the room. "We are expecting more people, and then we'll begin shortly."

The council looked around in confusion while my parents stared at me. I could read their energy; I didn't need to read anyone's thoughts. Queen Illeana was right; their energy was as clear as spoken words. My parents were proud, confused, and scared. They didn't know how to talk to me. A small part of them also wondered if I was still me.

Kagan returned shortly with a few people. "My queen, as you requested. Mr. Durham, your Marshal. He's in charge of your army." A tall, imposing man with a mustache and a crisp uniform came forward and kneeled on one knee. "My queen."

"It's nice to meet you, Mr. Durham. Please have a seat."

"Mr. Huxley, your castle steward. He's in charge of running the castle." A small, portly man with brown skin and glasses came forward and kneeled. "My queen."

"Pleasure, Mr. Huxley. Please have a seat."

"Mr. Adley, from the high courts," Kagan said and took his seat next to me.

"My queen," said a skinny man with long black hair tied in the back.

"Thank you, Mr. Adley. Please have a seat."

"I wanted to meet with you all to discuss the murder of Queen Illeana. I want to know what happened and who is responsible."

No one spoke. Uneasy eyes kept darting to my friends.

"Oh. I want to appoint Ciaran, Irina, and Kier as my advisors if they accept. Of course, I completely understand if you want to finish school first or if you want to think about it." I met each of their eyes to convey that they each had a choice.

"I accept," Irina said with a wink.

My lips quirked. I needed her by my side.

"Me too," Ciaran said.

I braced myself since I wasn't sure if Kier would accept. I wasn't even sure if keeping him close was fair to him or the quad, but I needed people I could trust next to me. I also wanted to make sure he was okay. I needed to be able to take away his sorrow or anything that wasn't normal within him. I wanted him to be free from my blood's influence. "Me three," Kier said.

"Excellent. Any other issues before we can proceed?"

When no one spoke, I addressed the council. "I was informed that you would know who was responsible for this."

Once again, they were silent. I could read the energy in the room. It was a mixture of fear, confusion, and protectiveness of me. They meant well, but they didn't understand that I wasn't Serris anymore. I was the queen, and they needed to be reminded of it, or we wouldn't be able to work side by side. "I'm not asking as your daughter or the child you watched grow up." I eyed my parents, then the other council. "I'm asking as your queen." My voice magnified, and I added some power to it.

"Forgive us, Queen Serris," Mr. Northwood said. "From what we gathered from previous attacks, everything points to the Fae."

"And have we confirmed this? Have we talked to the Fae?" *I needed Queen Illeana's book. I needed the librarian.* "Someone fetch the librarian for me, please." I realized I was confusing everyone, but this was important. We needed to act fast.

"Ah, my queen," Mr. Lazarus said carefully. "We spoke with the Fae, and the Seelie's swear it wasn't them. They are also doing their investigation. It could be the Unseelie."

I cocked my head as I gathered thoughts and memories about Unseelie. I wouldn't say I liked the knowledge I was receiving—they were powerful and dark.

"What about the creatures?"

"Creatures, my queen?" Mr. Durham asked.

My brow scrunched. "Were you not informed of my attack?"

"No, my queen."

I rubbed my temple. "I want everyone in this room informed of everything. I mean everything. Hold nothing back. Remember, I can read everyone's thoughts, so please don't disappoint me."

The door opened, and Liam came in with the librarian. A stout man with a friendly face and white hair. "My queen." He kneeled.

"Please stand." I tilted my head and found his name from my memories. "Borkin, I need Queen Illeana's book. Is it ready?"

His pudgy cheek twitched, and his face flushed red as fear surrounded him.

"You may speak freely." I forced a smile, but his fear was confusing. It tempted me to look inside his thoughts.

"I...It's just that." He kept his head bowed, then looked around the room helplessly. "I can't present the book to you, my queen, until the crowning ceremony." He dropped to his knees and bowed. "Please forgive me, my queen, but the magic won't activate unless it's presented during a ceremony."

"Is that it?" *Why is he so terrified*? I asked the quad.

Ser, don't get mad, but you're scaring everyone in the room. My gaze snapped to Colin. He met my eyes and shrugged. I raised my brow at Liam, and he nodded. *What am I doing?* I ignored it for now. I needed to focus on getting to the bottom of Queen Illeana's death.

"That's fine, Mr. Borkin. Thank you for explaining it to me. Please have it ready for the ceremony. We need it as soon as possible. How soon can we have the ceremony?" I asked Mr. Huxley.

"We had some preparations done, but it would still take at least a month to get everything in order."

"Unacceptable, we're having the ceremony tonight."

There was a commotion around the room, but no one voiced out their objection. "I sense that you don't all agree?" Irritation simmered under my skin. *Fuck, what was up with the emotional whiplash?* "I understand there are traditions. However, correct me if I'm wrong—the significance of the coronation was binding the queen to her position and her people. The ceremony is really just a formality more than anything. The purpose of it is to renew the magic by saying the oath. The rest is just for show. I want that ceremony done. I will give you until tomorrow to prepare. The death of our former queen is an act of war against our people, and I will not let it go unpunished." I pushed up from my seat. "If there is anything you need, ask my advisers or my mates. Until then, I expect to see you all at my ceremony."

I turned and flashed into the bedroom. I stripped the black dress off and crawled in bed with only my panties on. The power coursing through me felt terrifying and overwhelming. *I'm not ready for this.* I closed my eyes, and a tear fell on the pillow. The bed dipped, and Kagan was there, hovering over me. He wiped the tear with his thumb.

"Are you okay?"

I shook my head, and more tears came. I sat up, and the sheets uncovered my chest.

Kagan's gaze heated. I didn't move to cover myself. Instead, I waited to see what he would do. He stared at my breasts for a long time, then met my eyes. "You know I've loved you for a long time, Serris." My heart stuttered. "Since we were children, I've always been drawn to you, and each passing year, it grew more, much more, and I knew what I felt was real. It wasn't just the bond. It was overwhelming and obsessive, and it was almost scary." He bowed his head, and I saw regret in his eyes.

"I lasted maybe a week, the summer after we stopped speaking with you. I couldn't do it. I couldn't stay away from you. I had been by your side for as long as I could remember. Not seeing you for that long was like depriving myself of oxygen or water, something substantial I needed to live. I had decided to beg for your forgiveness, but then Jarius told me about the story of Queen Una and Queen Opal, and I couldn't take the risk." He drew in a breath and cupped my face. "I couldn't put my desires over your safety or risk weakening the bond." He chuckled darkly. "It wasn't all for nothing, though. When we were younger, I was a selfish prick. I didn't know how to share you with the others. I got jealous every time anyone touched you. In a way, the separation helped me. I think it had the same effect on the guys as well. We grew up knowing you were our mate, but we didn't know what that meant. The separation taught us we would get through it as long as you were in our lives. Anything was better with you in it." His lips touched mine; it was soft and felt like a shadow of a kiss. Something I could have imagined. Like he held himself back from it, like he wanted it, but thought he didn't deserve it. He kept my face between his hands and continued in a pleading tone. "The first thing I thought about every morning when I woke up was a solution of how to have you back in our lives without you knowing the truth, but I didn't find it, Serris. I'm sorry. I failed you and hurt you."

I leaned forward and captured his lips. His eyes grew in shock, his lips unmoving. I parted his mouth with my tongue, and soon he took over. He kissed me like he was a starving man eating his first meal. His passion reminded me of someone tasting a delectable delicacy he longed for but had never had before. His hand cupped my breast, and a growl rumbled from his chest. His muscles tensed, and he pulled away. "Serris, I can't. We can't start, or I won't stop. I have control of every aspect of my life except for you. With you, I can't seem to find an iota of control." He smiled and trailed kisses down my neck.

"Please don't stop. I'm tired of waiting, Kagan. I want to be with my mates." He eyed me, and I attacked his lips once again. He lay on top of me, the sheets long gone. His length rubbed against my panties, and I wrapped my legs around his waist to feel him. He paused and propped his elbows with his weight. "Are you sure?"

"There's so much power flowing through me, Kags. I could feel everyone. I feel like I'm slowly losing myself. I need you guys to remind me of who I am. I want to be with you. I need you." I reached up and kissed him.

"Serris, do you know what you're asking for? We have to be with you together, at least for the first time. It seals the mating bond. To do it one at a time risks one of us not being bonded to you."

"Is that why the others haven't fucked me?"

He chuckled. "Yes."

"I'm ready," I whispered.

"You know, you'll never be alone. We're always here to guide you and remind you. We'll be whatever you need us to be. Don't be afraid. You'll be a great queen, Serris."

I grabbed his face and kissed him, then whispered, "Please."

He cocked his head, and I knew he was communicating with the others. *Hmm, how can they block me out? Can I do that? Block some out when I want to?*

I didn't notice the twins flash inside the room until Kagan said, "Where's Godric?"

The door closed, and he answered, "I'm here. Are you sure, Serris?"

Kagan and I sat up. All eyes went to my naked chest. I wanted to roll my eyes, but I felt sexy from the way the quad all looked at me. Heat built in my stomach and an ache tingled between my thighs. "Yes." I breathed as I ran a hand down my stomach. The twins moaned.

"Get undressed and join me." The guys didn't need to be told twice as they quickly stripped naked and jumped in bed. I giggled, then froze when Kagan stripped naked. I'd never seen him naked before, and *wow*.

Godric was next, and I looked around the room, filled with awe. "How did I get so lucky?"

"We're the lucky ones, my love." Colin pulled my face to his and kissed me while Liam kissed my neck and shoulder. Kagan focused on my chest.

I squirmed, but Godric held both my legs down and ripped my panties off, then I felt his fingers between my folds, followed by his tongue. "Fuck, Yes." The sensation of my mates' hands and mouths were enough to drive me crazy, but I could also feel their emotions and desire, making it more intoxicating, bringing me to the edge. I crested higher and higher until I cried out in ecstasy.

Then I felt each of my mate's fangs sink into my skin, which took my orgasm to another level and had my body spasming and my eyes rolling back.

Can someone die from an orgasm? My mates took me to the peak each time they sucked on my blood.

When we finally joined our bodies, I was gone. I could only feel bliss and euphoria.

I discovered that my mates felt the same intense pleasure when I bit into their flesh as when they tasted my blood, so we spent the night having sex and taking each other's blood. They filled my body with bite marks. My mates were greedy and kept me awake all night; they devoured both my blood and my body until we passed out from exhaustion.

I woke up with a burning desire and four naked men with limbs tangled with one another. Colin rubbed my center, and Liam had my nipple in his mouth. I eyed the two and chuckled. "Haven't you two had enough?"

"Never," they said at the same time.

Colin kept up with his talented finger, which had me panting and squirming in no time. "I wouldn't mind having your blood for breakfast or every meal for eternity," Colin said with a heavy breath.

"Is it possible to be addicted to your mate's blood?" Liam asked in between kisses as he alternated between my breasts. "Tell me when."

"She's close," Colin said.

Colin pulled my legs down, which dislodged Kagan and Godric and entered me. I grunted from the sensation. In no time, I was riding an orgasm, which intensified as I felt Liam and Colin bite me. I bit into Colin and felt his release. I also heard Liam grunt out a release. "Fuck. I can come without touch, just from your blood," Liam said.

"Our turn, fuckers," Godric said.

I chuckled and sat on Kagan's lap as I slowly sank onto his shaft. He gripped my hips, and Godric pulled me to lean into him. His fingers flicked my nipples and my clit as I rode Kagan. "Bite me, baby," he whispered. I tilted my neck and bit below his ear. I could feel him build-up, which pushed me to the edge; soon, my muscles tensed, and Kagan bit into my breast, and I quivered my release, and Kagan grunted his at the same time.

"Are you sure you wanted that coronation today?" Colin asked.

"We can just spend all day in bed," Liam said.

It was freaking tempting. I considered it for a minute, but I had to bring justice to queen Illeana's death. "Don't tempt me. However, we have the motivation to finish early." I winked and sauntered into the bathroom.

I'm glad they didn't follow, or we would never make it out of the room. They were right. Now that we had sealed the bond, I could feel them with every fiber of my being. I no longer had doubts. I wanted my mates by my side at all times. More so, I needed them. It was fitting to have our lives tied together. I wouldn't want to live in a world without them.

Chapter 14
Serris

There was nothing special about the crowning. Only the heads, councils, the quad, and my advisers attended the private ceremony. After I said the oath, the crown was placed on my head. It was a thin, golden band with studded rubies. Then I was presented with a giant key that signified the key to the castle and the book. I asked everyone to stay for a moment to report what they knew about the attack.

I gained little information. So, I had been busy reading Queen Illeana's book, hoping to find a clue.

Kagan rubbed my shoulders, and I leaned back and moaned as the knots on my neck eased. "You've been reading for hours. Why don't you take a break?" He kissed my neck and down my shoulders.

"I can't. I need to find out who did this." I sighed. He continued to kiss both sides of my neck, and for a moment, I considered taking him up on his offer, but I knew once we got started, we wouldn't stop. I grabbed his face and pressed a kiss on his lips. "Soon, I promise," I said.

"Hurry, love. I'm impatient to be inside you," he whispered and kissed my neck, then left the study.

I clenched my legs together to tame my desire. *Fuck, that was hot.* After last night and this morning, our need for each other had become more potent. I could feel my mate's thoughts, feelings, and desires.

I needed to take care of this problem so I could enjoy my mates fully, so I immersed myself in the tome. My throat tightened when I read her entry of when she felt the first transfer of power. I couldn't even recall the incident. She talked about their plans to retire in a small, secluded cabin and enjoy a quiet life with her mates. I blinked the unshed tears away and used them to fuel my desire to avenge the queen. I kept reading, and finally, she wrote something about the Unseelie and Demons? *What the fuck?*

The quad flashed into the room, looking tense. "What is it?"

"Are you okay?"

Kagan's eyes traveled around the room, and I felt him cast a protection spell. Godric had his palms out, ready to blast his power.

"It's okay, guys. I just...read this." I pushed the book so they could see it.

"What the—?" Liam said.

"Are Demons real?"

"If the queen believes so and Serris had seen one, then they must be." Kagan's brow drew together in a serious expression.

"The queen fought a lot of them as well." I flipped the pages and showed them the entry.

They leaned forward, and their expressions grew tense as they read. Colin flipped the page, and his reaction morphed into confusion. He looked up to me in question.

"What?"

"The book went blank," he said.

"Oh. It's the enchantment. No one can read it but me. Apparently, I have to permit you each time." I shrugged and flipped the page for them to finish reading the entry.

"What are you going to do?" Kagan asked.

"I think it's time for me to meet with the rulers." I sighed. I wasn't ready to jump into politics, but I needed to get to the bottom of this.

Colin crossed his arms. "We need to finish the burial, and then we can arrange a meeting."

"When is the burial?"

"They have been holding off for as long as possible. They waited for you to wake up." Liam sat at the table.

"Okay, then let's have it tomorrow."

"We'll take care of it." Liam hopped off the desk.

"Thanks."

"Now, will you go to bed?" Colin walked around the desk and pulled me to my feet. He wrapped his arms around my waist and bent down to kiss me.

"Yes. I'm ready."

"Finally," Liam said as Colin swept my feet off the floor, and we blurred to the bedroom.

He tossed me onto the bed, which made me squeal.

"Serris, your bath is ready," Godric said from the door to the bathroom.

Colin leaned on the bed and groaned. I patted his head and said, "You could always join me."

He jumped up and carried me to the bathroom firefighter-style. I laughed, and he smacked me on the butt. I did the same, and he dumped me in the tub, fully clothed.

"You fucker." I pushed my wet hair off my face and stood up. "Because of that, you're not getting any." I stuck my tongue out.

The other guys laughed and joined me in the tub. Godric pulled me into his lap and helped me take off the rest of my wet clothing. Liam was still laughing and teasing Colin. "You can watch from the corner, brother."

"Serris, I'm sure I can change your mind," he said as he stripped slowly and flexed his muscles. He trained his heated gaze at me and smirked, which showed off his dimples, then grabbed his shaft and started rubbing himself. My breathing grew heavy as I watched him.

"Baby, I'm dying to be inside you. Can you see what you've done to me?" He breathed.

"Fine. You win, Colin," I said breathlessly. "Remember, two can play this seduction game."

"Yes," Colin smirked at Liam.

"You cheated, fucker." Liam splashed him with water.

We spent a relaxing time in the tub talking; it felt the same as when we were kids. Casual, not like the whole Vampire race rested on our shoulders.

I needed it. I was glad to have this part of my life still.

I stood above the stairs that overlooked the yard as I brushed a stray tear off my cheek. I stared at the queen's body on top of a pyre. On each side of her lay her mates. White flowers interspersed with red ones surrounded the queen. They dressed her in a black dress, and her mates wore black suits. *She looked peaceful like she was only sleeping.* Her black hair fanned out, and her full, red lips, along with her thick, black lashes, contrasted against her fair skin.

I felt a tug and squinted around the yard using my Vampire sight and studied the people that came to pay their respects to Queen Illeana. *We have a breach. Be on the lookout.*

Where? Kagan asked as he left my side. I was sure he went to direct Mr. Durham and his men.

I felt for the wards and sensed each Vampire in attendance. Vampires packed the place, but there were also some other races present. I touched everyone's energy and didn't feel anyone wanting to cause harm. I expanded my search outside of the castle grounds, and my chest flooded in coldness. Demons and Unseelie surrounded the castle. *Where are they coming from?* I closed my eyes to concentrate and sensed great energy close to the castle wall. I opened up my channels to my mates so they would know my thoughts.

I vaguely felt their panic and heard them jump into action. Godric stayed behind to protect the people inside the castle walls. Kagan directed the soldiers, and Liam and Colin stayed by my side as I flashed to the portal. I pulled immense energy from the Demons themselves to power the energy blast I used to attack the portal. I learned from Queen Illeana's journal how much power it took to destroy those fuckers, so I didn't mess around. It only took me three tries as I saw the portal crack and blast out. It helped that there were so many of them that surrounded the castle. I took their energy, so it would also weaken them at the same time. I waved my hand and protected the castle and my mates, which left the Demons and the Unseelie to take most of the blast.

These fuckers think they could disrupt Queen Illeana's burial? It isn't enough that they killed her! Not on my watch, fuckers. Irina, Ciaran, and Kier blurred to my side. "What do you need, Ser?" Kier asked.

I hesitated. It was too dangerous for them to be out here. Then our eyes grew as we watched the Demons and Unseelie recovering and some were making their way to the entrance. "Protect the entrance. Make sure no one gets through."

They nodded and blurred to the entrance.

There were too many. I looked around in panic. *How will we stop them?*

Liam had several Demons on the ground, writhing in pain or curled up and whimpering in front of me. I looked back and saw Colin had several Unseelie clutching their heads while blood gushed out of their eyes, nose, and ears. I needed to do something fast, but I was at a loss.

A dark, powerful man hidden under a cloak blasted my friends. Ciaran dropped to his knees as I saw his shield crack. Anger flared inside of me, hot as lava. I waved a hand and reinforced their shields. I thrust both my hands up and called on lightning. Dozens of lightning strikes came down on the Demons and Unseelie, and I heard sizzling and electricity buzz, then smelled burnt flesh as they screamed in pain.

The dark Unseelie lifted his head, and our eyes met. I saw hatred fill him, and I knew he was about to take off. I flashed in front of him and encased him with crushing energy that pulled on his life force. He struggled and tried blasting the bubble he was in, but it was no use. I made sure he powered his demise. *Payback's a bitch!*

I spread my hand and touched it to his face, which allowed me to speak with him. He wasn't the same dark Unseelie that attacked me, but they were similar. He had a deep scar running down from his left eye to his lip. He would have been handsome if it wasn't for the scar. He had a prominent nose and an angled jaw.

"Why do you keep attacking my people? What do you want?"

"Good one, young queen. I didn't think you had it in you. I underestimated you since you are new to your powers." He grimaced in pain and sagged onto the dome, but the energy kept him upright.

"What do you want from us?"

He struggled to speak, as he was on the brink of death. "It was nothing personal. I wish to reclaim what is mine. The true ruler of all." He said breathlessly.

I frowned and opened my mouth to ask what he meant. But then I flew a few feet and landed on my butt as I felt a searing pain in my shoulder and my stomach. The quad surrounded me.

"Serris." Kagan kneeled next to me.

"Are you okay?" Colin glanced at me briefly while he protected me.

"I'm fine. Just a gash," I hissed as Kagan healed my wounds. "Don't let him get away."

"I'm on it." Godric took off.

I stood on unsteady feet. "Ser, stop. I wasn't done." Kagan kept both hands on my waist.

I brushed him off and looked for Godric and the Unseelie. I saw two men surround the Unseelie, and together the three of them flashed out.

"No!" I raised a hand, but it was too late. I breathed hard, and my face contorted in anger. I threw fire after fire at all the remaining Demons and Unseelie.

"Serris, it's over. They're all gone," Irina said.

I slowly lowered my hand, and she wrapped her arms around Ciaran and me. Kier placed a hand on my shoulder. "Are you okay?"

I nodded and buried my face in my best friend's hugs. *I almost had him. The person responsible for the queen's death got away.*

You got him, love. I felt Colin's supportive energy.

Yes, he's weakened and at the brink of death. I doubt he could recover from that, Liam said.

No. He won't recover from that, Godric assured. He would know, since I attacked the Unseelie with something similar to his power.

Good.

We need to get back, Serris, Kagan said.

I flashed everyone back to the yard.

The Vampires clutched one another, and they filled the air with fear.

"No need to worry. We eliminated the threat. You are all safe."

One by one, the sea of Vampires kneeled and said, "My queen."

The sight and the emotion I felt from them was overwhelming. I felt humbled and honored. I also felt sadness since it somehow became more official that I was the queen of Vampires. I would no longer have a carefree life. I took a deep breath to shake off my sad thoughts and smiled. "Thank you. Your acceptance humbles me."

As long as I had my mates by my side, I would be fine. I felt the quad push their chorus of support. I grasped Kagan and Colin's hands, and I flashed my friends a smile. For a change, I wasn't afraid. I was ready.

Chapter 15
Serris

"Now that the oath has been renewed and you are aware of the repercussions. I don't need to tell you and your protectors what will happen if you break the oath." Lucian, the Shifter's ruler, said. I couldn't tell how old he was. Perhaps he was younger than he looked if it weren't for the scowl on his face. I didn't sense any animosity coming from him, so maybe it was just how he was.

"You called this meeting, Serris. How can we help you?" Katharina, the head coven witch, asked. Lucian's eyes darted to her, and his face softened. She noticed his gaze and kept her chin high, ignoring him. His eyes sparkled in amusement. *Something is going on between these two.*

"We were attacked during Queen Illeana's funeral. I captured the leader, and I believe he was also responsible for her death."

"Who is it?" Queen Aredhel asked. She looked pale, and the energy I sensed from her was weak. She was sick.

I studied her for a moment. She met my eyes, and I saw worry staring back at me. She minutely shook her head, and I understood she didn't want me to mention anything about her ailment. I inclined my head in a way no one would notice and answered, "I didn't know his name. He was Unseelie and had a scar running down his left eye."

There was an audible gasp around the room, and the Seelie queen's eyes grew, and the lines on her beautiful face deepened as she frowned.

"Are you certain? Perhaps it was someone similar?" Luca, the human ruler, said as he looked to the others.

"I don't know who he is. I could only describe him. He wore a black cloak where he hid his face."

"Then how did you see his scar?" Lucian interrupted.

I frowned at the worried glances they exchanged. "I captured him and weakened him. He was at the brink of death before two of his minions freed him."

"You captured the Unseelie king?" Aredhel said from behind her hand.

"You mean the man that killed Queen Illeana was the king of Unseelie?" I seethed, anger pouring out of me.

"You are filled with surprises, Queen Serris. We owe Queen Illeana a lot, and we are sad that she is gone. However, we are not disappointed that you have replaced her and are now part of our alliance. Please tell us what happened," King Luca said.

"As I said, he attacked during the ceremony, but I captured and weakened him. I drained his life force until he was on the brink of death. I asked him what he wanted with the Vampires, and he said he thought I would be weak since I just came into my powers. He said it was nothing personal, and he wanted to reclaim what was his. To be the ruler of all."

Everyone was silent. "That means he's coming after all of us," Katharina whispered.

"Will he recover from his injuries?" Aredhel asked.

"No, he was almost completely drained. Just a few more seconds and he would have been dead. Unless he has some unknown powers, he will not make a full recovery. Then again, he has command of unlimited numbers of Demons, so anything could be possible."

"We must be ready," Lucian said.

"Can someone please tell me who the king of the Unseelie is and why is he so determined to start a war?"

"His name is Sepitus Nox, and he ruled the Unseelie with a heavy hand. He admired his great grandfather, who started the great war. He was rumored to have other races under his command. Those that were unwanted or unhappy with their ruler found refuge in his realm. His father was once part of this council, but once he took command, he absconded. We didn't hear from him for a long time until the attacks happened. We were unaware of who was responsible. We thought it was an unknown race since we've never encountered Demons before. Sepitus believes that the Fae are the true rulers of both earth and faery since all races came from them."

"Not humans," Luca snarled.

"That's why he hates humans the most," Lucian said.

"He had always been interested in dark magic," Katharina said.

"I don't expect he would surface anytime soon if he truly were injured. It would take a while for him to recover if he could," Aredhel said.

"What do you propose we do?" I asked. "I don't think we should sit idly by and allow him to recuperate. Let us find him while he's weakened."

"I like her." Lucian grinned.

Katharina glared at him, and he bowed his head in response. I hid a smile as I watched the two.

"I agree. I'll investigate the first attack. Illeana said there was a Shifter involved?" Lucian asked.

"No, I think I should investigate," Katharina interrupted.

"Why you?" Lucian frowned.

"Because it's your people. We need an impartial person investigating."

"It's precisely the reason I should do it."

"Children." Luca massaged his temple. "Must we go through this every single time? Katharina should do it, and Lucian will assist. Raise your hand if you agree."

We all raised our hands except for Katharina and Lucian, who glared at each other.

"Since that's settled, I'll start looking for Sepitus in Faery," Aredhel said.

"It might take time before he makes another move. We might get lucky and find him in his weakened state. However, given his past, I doubt we will. In the meantime, stay vigilant. We are officially at war with the Unseelie, and we need to be careful and protect all races from Demons." Luca pushed off his seat and stood. "If there is nothing else to discuss. I will depart and make sure our wards are strong. Let's keep close contact if there's another attack." He nodded and departed.

I looked around and watched everyone else do the same.

Well, that was interesting.

Yeah, they're efficient. You can't doubt that. Colin chuckled.

What now? Liam asked.

Now, we prepare and wait. Let's hope we don't hear from this crazy king for a long time, Kagan said.

Let's hope one of the royals takes care of him before he becomes our problem. Godric wrapped his arms around me as Kagan flashed us back to the castle.

"I guess that leaves us with time." I shrugged.

"What did you want to do with your time?" Colin wiggled his brows.

I laughed. "I don't know. I was told I could renovate the castle. I could always learn how to be a queen. I guess."

"Boring. How about we stay in the bedroom for about a month and not leave?" Liam pulled me into his lap.

"I like that as well," I whispered as I wrapped my arms around his neck.

I smiled as excitement filled me. For the first time in several years, I looked forward to spending time with my mates.

T HE END

W ant to read more about the other rulers? Order the next book in the next page.

Also by Lina Bengston
High Priestess

How come I attract the worst types of men?
    I am the high priestess of a caster race, and I cannot be attracted to the pompous King Shifter.

A mighty Unseelie king is determined to rule all supernatural races and wipe out humans. He organized an attack that ended with the death of the vampire queen. While we know the culprit, it surprised us to learn that he had allies from our own race.

I shouldn't have volunteered to investigate the suspect because I have to work closely with the Wolf King. Worse still, the suspect is not a lone wolf but another alpha-hole that is perhaps worse than the king. Who, of course, makes me boil with rage and desire.

Needless to say, they make my job very difficult.

I hope we solve the mystery of who is a friend or enemy of our people before facing the battle we all fear.

High Priestess is a standalone paranormal romance series where the heroine doesn't have to choose. The novel includes light bullying themes and adult scenes.

King's Heirs

Holy hot shifters!

Who would have thought supernaturals existed? Not only are they real, but I'm one of them—an heir to shapeshifters.

Now I must attend a magical academy and join the king's heirs. Many students, including the heirs, were not happy to learn about me. Not only am I an anomaly, but female heirs are unknown, which makes me a supernatural target.

Just as the heirs were warming up, the witches and vampires intervened. Now, my powers are acting strangely, which makes me rethink whether I was an heir or something different. I must discover what makes me different and master my powers before my enemies get to me.

This is a fast-burn, fated mate romance where the heroine doesn't have to choose.

Violence, Foul language, and Adult content included.

Other Pen Names: P.C. Benson: Paranormal Romance/Urban Fantasy Author

M^{ated}

A fter many lifetimes of solitude, my mate is here at last. Four years ago, I jolted awake by scorching energy flowing through me as the Savior's soul claimed mine. After several millennia, my wait is over—she's finally here.

Her arrival, however, foreshadowed a war between the Nephilim and the Fallen.

Since then, I've traveled the world in search of her, but she's been elusive. I know she's near—I feel her in my soul.

However, time is running out. I need to find her and keep her safe, regardless of the cost, since she's the key to saving us all.

This is the second edition of the Nephilims' Savior. The first edition appeared under a different title, another cover and some sections were rewritten.

Don't miss out!

Visit the website below and you can sign up to receive emails whenever Lina Bengston publishes a new book. There's no charge and no obligation.

https://books2read.com/r/B-A-MMVM-RMAQB

BOOKS 2 READ

Connecting independent readers to independent writers.